CW00495592

WITCHING GAMES

THE FIRE WITCH CHRONICLES: 1

R.A. LINDO

PERIUM PUBLISHING

CONTENTS

AUTHOR'S NOTE

The Fire Witch Chronicles is a spin-off series, following a character from the **Kaira Renn Series.**

There's no need to read the Kaira Renn Series, but please be aware there are some references to the original series.

WELCOME TO A MAGICAL UNIVERSE

Welcome to the secret, magical universe of **The S.P.M.A. (The Society for the Preservation of Magical Artefacts.)**

If you want to delve deeper into the magical universe of the S.P.M.A., **sign up** to become eligible for free books, private giveaways and early notification of new releases.

You can also join **my private Facebook group** where all things S.P.M.A. are discussed.

Founders' Quad Map

Society Square Map

1

THE FIRE WITCH

Society Square buzzes with activity as the hordes of shoppers stare in a mixture of puzzlement and wonder at the array of buildings: all linked to a secret, magical Society of course, but the above-ground world remains none the wiser.

I stand on the church roof, hidden from view, smiling at families approaching Leaning Lane famous for the way its buildings decrease in size. A small, powder-blue bird buzzes near my shoulder; a special bird with the ability to shape-shift. It's called a Williynx and can breathe ice, but more on that later.

The children drag their parents towards Wimples sweet shop: the sweets people drive across the country to get their hands on ... strange sweets that leave impressions on the tongue ... moving illustrations of the figure on the packets. The names of the sweets are another draw for the kids ... *Codswollops* and *Core Blimeys* ... all part of the wonder of Wimples sweet shop, causing howls of laughter from crowds of children gathered outside.

The laughter fills the air, reminding me of a time not so

long ago when that was me: an innocent girl having no idea of the wonders hidden beneath the sleepy, English town of Bibsley Corbett.

That was before my mum dropped the bombshell on my brother's eighteenth birthday ... that she worked in a place called The Cendryll: a faculty in a vast, magical universe known as The Society for the Preservation of Magical Artefacts (S.P.M.A. for short). I remember bursting out with laughter at the news.

"Magic *doesn't exist*," I recall saying in my particularly insolent manner.

My mum didn't respond to my comment, only that we needed to get ready. She wasn't the warmest of people then and has gone through a pretty big transformation since. Needless to say, I found out magic *did exist* and, before long, met a girl called Kaira. We became firm friends and went on a magical, mystery tour through all the amazing buildings and magical realms, soon realising that all was not well.

My brother, Jacob, joined us on our adventures, becoming the voice of reason to manage our madcap plans. Well, mainly *my* madcap plans. Conrad's arrival took things to another level: the lost boy who discovered a particular gift whilst capturing the heart of a certain girl: me.

Me? I'm Guppy Grayling. 16 years old, 5ft 5inches, brown hair, all-black attire. Not your average Night Ranger but, then again, my entrance to this magical world was out of the ordinary, to say the least. Night Rangers are Society soldiers tasked with keeping law and order. Weapons are important for the role, my weapon of choice being swords formed from a special type of morphing steel known as a Vaspyl: steel that can form into any object imaginable.

Friends call me Guppy but most people know me as The Fire Witch, mainly because of the way I appear when trouble's brewing. I like to burst through a ball of fire, reminding questionable figures that I survived the curses of one of the most feared wizards in our magical universe.

My dramatic arrival normally does the trick, but there's always someone lurking in the shadows who needs more persuading. That's where the magic of battle comes in: all hidden from above-ground eyes, of course.

Along with my swords, I've got plenty of charms at my disposal: investigative, protective and defensive charms, not to mention the ability to counteract dark magic (Gorrah). There's been little evidence of dark deeds since the recent war, but no-one in the S.P.M.A. is naïve enough to think malevs aren't roaming in the shifting realms beyond The Society Sphere.

Malevs are the ones I keep an eye on — ex-communicated members usually up to no good. More mischief than malice because they've learnt where betrayal leads: a trip across Quibbs Causeway to send them mad or, worse, into the bowels of The Velynx where they rot in slime-filled cells.

As I stand on the church roof, hidden by an invisibility charm, I think about Kaira — my best friend and the daughter of the all-powerful Casper Renn who remains in charge of The Cendryll. Kaira will be forever linked to wild adventures and the hunt for a dark wizard and an evil artefact, but she's chosen a quieter life for now, journeying through the more serene places of the S.P.M.A., deciding Society duties can wait.

My brother, Jacob, has taken on a teaching role in The Cendryll, tasked with educating The Fateful Eight in all things magical. The Fateful Eight is the name given to the eight children chosen to join each faculty: a trial agreed by the Society elders to honour the principle of beauty and unity many fought and died for. Until my arrival, no under eighteens were allowed and the S.P.M.A. was *all* about secrecy.

Needless to say, *that* backfired when the secret hunt for the most evil artefact in existence gathered pace, leading to a sudden crisis in the Society, and a realisation that secrecy and marginalisation were counterproductive. In the end, it took a group of kids and the marginalised species in the Society to battle evil, restoring peace.

Beauty and unity has become the S.P.M.A.'s motto ever since, meaning you're as likely to see a young wizard as you are an ageing giant. You'll also find magical creatures in all faculties: spectacular, shape-shifting birds along with tiny, luminous insects known as Quij.

The sky urchins are still learning the ropes, refusing to replace their black rags covering their scar-ravaged bodies for something more fitting. Their scars are marks of war, they argue — wars fought for the Society's survival and something that should never be forgotten.

The morning mist rests over Society Square, washing Founders' Quad with muted light. It's my favourite vantage point, partly because it's a reminder of the old days when innocent wonder dominated, but also because it's become a meeting point for romantic flight.

The romantic part is linked to Conrad — the boy I slowly fell for on our journey towards a maelstrom of danger two years ago. I remember how quiet he was at first, appearing in The Cendryll with a sullen expression, struggling with a sadness hanging over him.

He didn't have the best introduction to the S.P.M.A., bumping into Erent Koll in his first few days: the dark wizard who destabilised the Society. Conrad's a different prospect now: tall, confident and handsome — the mild scars running across his chest and arms adding a reminder of what he's lost.

He's learnt not to dwell on the past too much, realising the importance of appreciating the wonder of the magical world we're blessed to be part of. From my vantage point on top of the church roof, I'm reminded of the life I once had, walking with the crowds through the streets of Founders' Quad, grasping for moments of excitement to counteract the boredom of my life.

The eight children selected for entrance to each faculty are about to experience the same awe and wonder, soon to be stunned by the *impossibility* of the universe they've been granted entrance to — a universe that is multi layered, offering portals to all things magical. Portals are called Periums in the S.P.M.A., and I wait for the boy I love to arrive through one hidden in the sky.

Conrad is about to appear on the back of a beautiful, turquoise, bird: a majestic, shape-shifting creature. Like me, he'll be hidden from view with an invisibility charm, knowing the consequences of using magic above ground. Conrad's a sky rider now, joining me on my evening pursuits as a Night Ranger.

We keep an eye on things from the skies, the trick of invisibility is created by the Verum Veras charm: a glimmering curtain of protection allowing undetected movement. As I wait behind my curtain of invisibility, I feel my bracelet vibrate on my right wrist — my penchant allowing me to travel through a world of wonder.

Conrad appears seconds later, spinning through the sky above me as a glittering curtain of gold light surrounds him, gliding down on his turquoise Williynx for our morning rendezvous. The burning sensation inside returns every time I see him: the boy with copper-blonde hair and a dazzling smile.

I barely noticed boys before Conrad but, then again, I barely noticed *anything* until I stepped into The Society for the Preservation of Magical Artefacts. My mum mastered the art of neglect a long time ago, so it was just me and Jacob keeping ourselves entertained at home.

Now, there's entertainment at every turn from — a simple charm generating showers of light or a vanishing act to another spectacular space. Night Rangers need their fun too, though, the reason Conrad and I meet here each morning. The morning meetings give us our 'alone time' before duty calls, ready to transport us to other magical realms.

"Hey," he says as his Williynx touches down on the church roof — the shimmering curtain of protection keeping a unique vision hidden from view. After all, a boy appearing out of the sky on the back of a huge turquoise bird would be pretty hard to explain.

I give Conrad the once over, always drawn to the scar lining his neck ... the scar I know runs diagonally across his torso ... gained from an attack of vampiric birds in a land once housing evil. We survived that battle, recovering in our own way, ensuring every available moment is spent experiencing new wonders.

I've got my own scars, decorating my wrists and lower legs. Conrad says he likes them ... that it reminds him of how we met and the unique things we've gone through. I doubt that, but it doesn't matter. He's here and he's mine and, for now, that's all I need.

"Where to?" he asks, running a hand through his hair. The white T-shirt, grey coat and jeans do little to protect him from the cool temperatures, but he's long been conditioned against the elements.

"You choose," I reply, kneeling to place my right hand on the ground, whispering 'Expandeus' as I do so. The charm causes my invisibility charm to stretch outwards and upwards ... the glimmering, golden curtain of protection expanding with my powder-blue companion ... the small bird buzzing near my shoulder now shape-shifting into a glorious form more fitting for a Williynx.

I climb on as my Williynx settles, resting its head on the concrete floor of the church roof. With a shimmering curtain of golden dust hovering around us, I glance at Conrad, signalling the race is on.

"I might let you win this time," I offer with a flirtatious smile. We've got time for a little closeness before the morning mist gives way to a clearer light, illuminating the wistful and wayward.

Looking up at the tunnel of glimmering light lining our way to the portal in the sky , Conrad returns the smile. "First one above the clouds gets to choose where we visit."

"Fair enough," I say, placing my face in my winged companion's powder-blue feathers. The feeling of flying is infinitely better with your eyes closed ... the exhilaration rushing through your body as you ascend at speed ... made even better with the boy you love beside you.

"Then we free fall into the place we're visiting," Conrad adds with a sly grin, knowing he's the master of this particular trick. "Don't worry," he continues, "I'll catch you if you lose control."

I study his face and lean torso, *fully planning* to lose control to make the most of our morning rendezvous.

"I'll give you a head start," I add before he leans in for a kiss, and then he's gone, darting upwards through the golden tunnel of light, hiding us from above-ground eyes ... a vision of love I race to catch as my powder-blue Williynx swirls silently upwards, acutely aware that any display of magic outside of our secret world comes with severe consequences.

As I fly through the sky, keeping my body pressed to my Williynx, I turn and look down at the dots moving through Society Square. The above-ground crowds have no idea of the magical universe hiding in plain sight, existing in the fabric of the very shops they're visiting now — too conditioned in the mundane to question the bizarre offerings in shops like Wimples and The Spinning Shoe.

Feeling the buzz of my penchant as we near the spinning portal in the sky, I smile at how lucky I am: an ordinary girl in an extra-ordinary world about to embark on another day of adventure.

2

THE WINTER QUARTER

We glide through the portal in the sky, spinning through the glittering tunnel of multi-coloured light until we re-appear, overlooking The Winter Quarter. This part of The Society Sphere is famous for its gentle light and endless snow. The light washes streets and buildings forming the above-ground section — the snow a strange wonder for those lucky enough to access magical spaces.

We'll make a dramatic arrival in the next few minutes, appearing to track a certain person who is making a few too many trips to The Shallows: a place where a certain evening witch is said to be hanging out. For now, though, I enjoy the feeling of the snow falling on my face as Conrad itches to begin our romantic ritual.

His intensity is one of the most attractive things about him ... an intensity I feel every time he makes eye contact, as if he's studying something deep within me. He wasn't always this adorable, by the way, and it would be fair to say I found him a bit *limp* when he first arrived in The Cendryll, but I was less trusting then and he'd recently lost his mum.

He's now lost both parents, adding to his brooding energy, but somewhere along the way he decided to park his grief and immerse himself in the wonder at his fingertips.

As the wind lifts my long, brown hair, a single powder-blue feather falls from my Williynx followed by a turquoise one from Conrad's feathered companion: a sign our romantic ritual is about to begin. We arrive in the magical realm of The Winter Quarter, snow falling softly on our faces as we glide side-by-side.

"Ready...?" Conrad asks.

I nod, lowering my face into my Williynx' coat of powder-blue feathers before a tap of my feet causes an explosion of feathers, marking the beginning of the race. With the snow falling onto the Williynx' colourful coats, we spin in tandem as we dart through the sky, Conrad staying low on his turquoise companion, urging it forward.

The vision of the snow falling in gentle patterns is one I never tire of, savouring the tranquil beauty of the space we fly within. Not too long ago, we were journeying in unknown territory, hunting evil things and evil people. Now, it's more about fun with the odd journey to strange realms.

With the race on, I whisper to Laieya — the name of my Williynx - as I edge ahead of Conrad, blowing him a sarcastic kiss as I do: a reminder that the girl he's fallen for can more than hold her own.

With the race over and me victorious, we glide lower until the buildings come into clearer view. The sight of vast, colourful creatures carrying Society members isn't anything out of the ordinary in Society spaces, The Winter Quarter being no exception.

This can't be said for free falling ... the art of spinning off your Williynx in a rapid, kamikaze descent. The Society elders frown on such elaborate acts, but Conrad and I agree we've earned the right to bend the rules. We got dragged into a war we helped to end, eradicating significant threats for the Society's benefit, so a little bit of drama in the sky should be allowed.

"Remember to hold on if you spin out of control," teases Conrad, preparing for the rapid descent.

I feign helplessness as my powder-blue Williynx lets out an almighty squawk and then I'm gone, spinning free from Laieya as I hurtle towards the ground. I know how to regain control of my spinning body but enjoy the sensation of syncing with Conrad as we fall ... a simple act of alignment beginning with hands connecting before our legs entwine.

The seemingly perilous fall takes on balletic tones as we enact our hilarious sky dance, exaggerating each twirl and extension until the ground nears and our Williynx swoop down to our rescue, delivering us to snow-covered streets on the trail of a shifty figure engaging in secretive travel.

~

WITH OUR WILLIYNX WAITING OUTSIDE, ADAPTING THEIR forms to perch on street lamps, I take out a vial of purple liquid and gulp it down in one go: Fillywiss for the senses, helping to restore equilibrium. Society crowds fill the snow-covered streets, decorated in a various array of clothing, some more elegant than others. The landscape of this winter wonderland is marked by a shimmering, sinking bridge — one of its unique features — the other being perpetual snow.

The bridge is for magical travel, allowing members swift access to different realms. It's a different sort of Perium, offering a novel way of moving between various parts of the S.P.M.A.

The pub we're heading to sits at the foot of the bridge — a raucous place full of lost souls and Society folk with little waiting for them at home. My weapons of choice won't be needed on this visit which is basically assessing movements and interactions. There's no threat of danger, and the ramshackle wizard in question is no warrior.

Joseph Flint is a gentle soul obsessed with Society facts. He can be normally found talking to himself inside The Chattering Tap, mumbling obscure magical facts to an invisible companion. Until now, Joseph has been gently mad, but his sudden visits to The Shallows via The Sinking Bridge suggest he's formed a bond he'd prefer to keep secret.

WE ENTER THE CHATTERING TAP AND MAKE OUR WAY TO AN empty table, giving us a good view of Joseph. Familiar faces nod in greeting, forever grateful for all we did to win the war two years ago. It's amazing what a battle with a bad wizard can do for your status, particularly when the concept of an underage wizard fighting in battle had previously been derided.

With our Williynx in view outside — smaller in stature to put the more nervous witches and wizards at ease — large glasses of multi-coloured liquid are slammed on the tables by the proprietors: a family of seven, including the pretty girl who always eyes Conrad when we're here.

"Hey, handsome," Lorina Lellant says in Conrad's direction, followed by a flirtatious smile.

Conrad offers a forced smile in return, aware of how I feel about Lorina. They don't call me The Fire Witch for nothing.

"Still popular then," I tease, accepting the boy blessed

with beauty and a warrior spirit is going to get female attention.

I ignore the stare Lorina gives me, glancing over at the group of wizards attempting to demonstrate the combined powers of certain magical powders. As the pink, yellow and red powders are blown from one wizard's hand, the group stands back to wonder at the fizzing sphere of multi-coloured light forming above them — the beginnings of a new charm it seems.

That's until it begins to spin out of control, causing the clientele to duck for cover. Conrad's the first to stand on the table, whipping out the Weveris charm as he sends a web floating towards the erratic sphere of light. I step onto the table alongside him, uttering 'Disira' the moment Conrad's web ensnares the fizzing force rebounding off the walls and windows.

It explodes as my disintegration charm makes contact, causing a shower of sparks to fall over the pub like confetti: our introductory act for the evening. After a light round of applause, we return to our seats only to find Joseph Flint has left his place at the bar.

I study the snow-covered streets outside, spotting his parked car ... a battered contraption parked outside on the opposite side of the street. He's obviously sensed the reason for our presence and made his exit, but not following his recent pattern via The Sinking Bridge.

"He's gone above ground," states Conrad, standing and buttoning his grey coat. "We can't use magic there so will need to use Periums to track his location."

I adjust the belt on my black leather trousers, having a good idea of the route Joseph is going to take. Any shifty movement is studied closely by wizards and witches on the ground, and a variety of creatures in the sky, including Williynx and sky urchins.

It's in everyone's interest to avoid another war: a unified Society more powerful than a fragmented one. Joseph isn't likely to ignite a war any more than he's likely to attempt an attack on his fellow wizards and witches. He *is* up to something, though, and his little escape plan only serves to reinforce this.

"You take the streets; I'll take the sky," suggests Conrad as we exit The Chattering Tap.

"Yep," I agree, gesturing for my Williynx to reduce its form even further, ready to step through a different Society building and into the soft light decorating the above-ground section of The Winter Quarter. "See you in The Shallows," I offer in a parting gesture to Conrad, along with a quick kiss. He always smells good and I'd like to stay close to his scent, but all good things ...

Kneeling to signal his Williynx into action, Conrad adds, "I'll meet on the other side of The Sinking Bridge, where Joseph will probably appear. Then I get my own revenge in our race back to The Cendryll."

I step in closer, inhaling his scent for a little longer before reminding myself of the task at hand. "Injured pride?" I tease as he pulls me towards him.

"Something like that," he offers, those green eyes working their own magic and then he's off, bursting into the sky astride his turquoise companion — the single feather floating towards me always making me smile.

I SPOT JOSEPH FLINT FROM THE UPPER FLOOR OF ROEYLIN'S: A tall, narrow building crammed with toys. Like Wimples sweet shop, it's a natural attraction for children who are awe struck by the unique toys on offer. Quite *how* they work doesn't matter to them — magic, of course — and parents end up paying just to get their kids *out* of the shop, putting up with flying, buzzing, battery-powered devices that seem to have a life of their own.

The upper floor of Roeylin's is a quieter affair, designated as Staff Only. The staff in question are Society members, as they are in all buildings within The Society Sphere. From here, I have sight of Joseph, able to close in on him via one of the doors situated in each corner of the room.

All four doors are black and decorated with a brass handle. Those in the know pull the door handle out and twist it until the desired destination appears in gold lettering. You need a penchant for this to work: an item of jewellery usually decorated by a gemstone.

The Grayling penchant stone is topaz blue; Conrad's tanzanite. I step to the door nearest to the window and pull the brass handle back, feeling the usual spinning sensation as if I'm losing my footing. The feeling of dizziness passes and I study the gold letters appearing above the door handle, waiting for Babberley's Barbers to appear.

It's the shop nearest to Joseph's current position, and the one he's about to enter to get to The Shallows: a strange place located beyond The Society Sphere. He's up to something there, recently making it a daily routine. *No one* needs to visit The Shallows every day unless they're Night Rangers like me, checking in on shifty characters.

Joseph Flint isn't a Night Ranger or, until now at least, not shifty in the slightest, but his usual mutterings to invisible companions in The Chattering Tap have increased in intensity, suggesting a wizard on the edge — caught up in things he shouldn't be.

With my Williynx in the form of tiny bird, I step through the door when my location appears, pushing the brass door handle as I do, happy to see a familiar slide glittering in the colour of my penchant stone, leading me to my destination and the man about to be tracked to his mysterious contact in The Shallows.

3

THE SHALLOWS

I appear in a barber's chair in a tiny room with only one distinguishing feature: a peephole on the white brickwork ahead of me. Looking into the peephole is the first step, causing the barber's chair to edge closer. Once my right eye is pressed against the white bricks, I wait for wooden stairs to appear before the peephole expands and I'm sucked through ... my feet resting at the top of a staircase.

Most forms of magical travel aren't as complicated as this, but some places in the S.P.M.A. have added security, mainly for particularly unique realms and those presenting a *challenge*. For example, the staircase I'm standing on now rises and twists into a formidable beast if it senses bad intentions. *Challenge*, by the way, is a euphemism for danger, Society elders preferring not to use the D word.

As blessed as our mercurial breed is, not all of us have the courage to match our magical gifts, meaning any whiff of danger usually triggers an exodus to gentler realms. The Shallows don't fall into the 'gentle' category so I take precautions, retrieving a device from my leather trousers: a Follygrin.

Bound in leather, a Follygrin can track anyone at the mention of a few words: *Ask and You Will Find*. So I ask and the pages flick to the letter J ... causing an intricate, moving illustration to form of the wizard in question ... currently being lifted into the air by a carpet formed of white weeds.

Joseph Flint jumps from one moving object to another until he propels himself forwards, vanishing out of sight. I know where's he's headed now, making my way down the staircase towards a land of floating objects and shifting earth — on the track of an eccentric wizard seemingly up to no good.

WITH LAIEYA RETURNING TO A MORE MAJESTIC FORM, I REACH the bottom of the steps and enter The Shallows, glancing up at the sky for any sign of Conrad. Many things move up above, including the carpets of white weeds, transporting the traveller onwards.

Conrad won't be alone up there — the sky urchins an ever present force in all realms beyond The Society Sphere. Now an intrinsic part of the S.P.M.A., the scar-ravaged creatures are designed for battle, meaning whilst they view it as an honour to be welcomed into Society faculties, The Wenlands will always be their home.

I'M HOPING THE SKY URCHINS WON'T BE NEEDED THIS morning. The plan is to maintain subtle surveillance — the role of Night Rangers unless, of course, there's more than mischief at work out here. Remaining invisible will help, so as I call a carpet of weeds towards me I whisper 'Verum Veras', the glittering curtain of light forming around me.

Conrad will hover high in the sky, out of sight, until I close in on Joseph which is when closer surveillance begins. With the glittering curtain of protection surrounding me, I get my balance as I step onto the floating platform, leading me towards the jump Joseph Flint made moments ago and the mystery figure whose company he's so keen to keep.

With other floating forms gliding past me, I whistle to my Williynx before jumping into the swirling atmosphere of light ... reappearing on the other side of a moving landscape. The land moves like a collection of rivers, the soil bending and twisting in various directions towards different parts of The Shallows.

Once you get to your destination, the earth dips into a steep incline, offering a panoramic view of the district you've arrived at. I'm guessing Joseph is headed to Poridian Parlour: a place where weary wizards and witches gather. There's a certain someone said to be hiding out there—someone I'd love to reacquaint myself with: Alice Aradel aka the evening witch.

Alice Aradel picked the wrong side in the last war, leaving her crew to scatter far and wide, desperate to avoid a trip along Quibbs Causeway: the mind-altering path where the Mantzils live. The Mantzils are invisible creatures able to unhinge the mind: a slice of evil not vanquished in the battle with Erent Koll: The Prince of the Underworld.

As my brother, Jacob, once said: it's naïve to hope for a world without evil — even a magical one — which is why Night Rangers and Society soldiers will always be needed, even when everything seems calm on the surface. If my guess is right, Alice Aradel's got a hold over Joseph, identifying his weaknesses and making him pay for it ... or so she thinks.

At the sight of a faint shower of light above me — the signal of Conrad's descent into action — I ready my weapons through the command of 'Comeuppance'. Taking out two steel objects from my leather trouser pocket, I throw them into the air, imagining two silver swords, and they transform into just that ... the handles falling gently into my hands. The artefact is a Vaspyl, better known as morphing steel.

Alice Aradel might be the evening witch, but I'm *The Fire Witch* and she's about to meet an old foe, ready to transport her to the very place she fears: The Velynx. The Velynx is a place for bad things and bad people, Alice Aradel falling neatly into this category. Wanted for crimes including theft of rare artefacts and attempted kidnap (of me), she must be pretty desperate to have to call on Joseph Flint for help.

I blink to clear my vision after passing through the sphere of light, keen for Conrad to appear. The single turquoise feather signifies his arrival before he dismounts, walking alongside me with his own weapons at the ready ... energy as opposed to mass in the form of fireballs spinning around his arms and wrists. It looks like Alice Aradel is in for the surprise of her life.

With his feathered companion joining mine, gliding in the air above us, Conrad fixes his gaze ahead. "Do you think it's her?" he asks in reference to Alice Aradel.

"Possibly. Who else would have got into Joseph's head?"

"He's fragile," Conrad adds, ever conscious of the mistake his dad made.

"He is," I agree, enjoying the thrill of tracing danger. "Let's just hope he hasn't done anything stupid."

"If he's caught up with Alice Aradel, he would've been

put up to it," Conrad states. "She's got a way of putting the frighteners on people."

"Not on me."

"Me neither, but Joseph isn't built for battle; he's never recovered from the death of his sister."

I say nothing to this, familiar with the nature of grief. Conrad's been taken to places I haven't, though, having lost his mum and dad in the space of a few months. He's right — Joseph Flint is broken and needs to be extracted from anything he's caught up in, meaning whoever's holding him to ransom is about to feel the heat of a witch's fire.

Creating his own invisibility charm, Conrad allows his arms to fall by his side, allowing the fireballs swirling around his hands to fade to a temperate glow. Our weapons may or may not be needed, but no trained warrior steps beyond The Society Sphere unarmed. Peace might have returned to the S.P.M.A. but that still leaves Melackin, malevs and black market rats to keep an eye on: 'the triad of trouble' I like to call them.

Malev is short for malevolent (meaning malicious and spiteful) whilst Melackin are rehabilitated wizards: my mum falling into *that* category. Black market rats are the shifty group that survive by trading of harmless objects, like Sootherals that send children to sleep in seconds. *Every* above ground parent is after a Sootheral, travelling to Society Square from all over England in search of the precious device.

No magical artefact is supposed to end up in the hands of above-ground folk, but perfection doesn't exist in any world: magical or otherwise. As long as the questionable ones among us aren't putting the Society in danger, the elders don't lose too much sleep over it. I should probably mention now that 'the elders' are the people who debate procedures, but it's The Orium Circle who make all the laws.

Made up of six people, The Orium Circle are the most senior witches and wizards in the S.P.M.A. I know one of them particularly well — Weyen Lyell — the wizard with the wicked afro who survived a blistering war in The Saralin Sands.

As our Williynx spread out their vast wings, offering further protection, Conrad points to the figure entering Poridian Parlour.

"I doubt he's travelling every day to have tea and cake," he says, whistling for his Williynx to shape-shift into a smaller form: a necessary action in a space where peace and tranquility is the general rule.

The soil twists and turns in various directions, representing each traveller's path. Each footprint has the S.P.M.A. logo emblazoned in the soil — one of the conditions of Society members moving within and beyond The Society Sphere.

Anyone thinking of doing anything *really stupid* can be tracked via their footprint ... the S.P.M.A. logo within the footprint carefully cut out of the soil and placed into a Nivrium — better known as a water reader.

If the intent is bad or unclear, surveillance is placed on the figure in question, which is where Night Rangers come in. Casper Renn has put a surveillance order on Joseph Flint.

'Subtle surveillance' was how he put it, knowing me too well, although subtlety isn't my strong point. I mean, what's the point of being The Fire Witch if you can't have a little fun?

"So, fire for your entrance or something a little more low key?" Conrad asks with a smile: *those eyes*. He's jokingly referring to my chosen mode of entrance, wondering if I'm going to appear from the invisibility charm or activate the Smekelin charm to burst through a wall of flames.

"That depends on who Joseph's wining and dining, although fire always makes people spill the beans."

"Well," Conrad adds, "try not to burn the place down this time."

"That was only once," I counter, loving how my leather trousers complete my witchy look. Jacob tells me the handful of Society kids he's teaching think I'm a vampire. Stories of me sleeping in the day and moving at impossible speed fill his classroom, making me want to drop by to release a flurry of Ameedis: vampiric birds to reinforce the myth. Jacob doesn't think that's a good idea; I tell him he's lost his sense of humour

"We enter unseen and strike if necessary," Conrad suggests, reigniting his balls of fire within the glittering curtain of protection, keeping us out of sight as we near the region resting in a quarry, buildings bursting out in every direction. Some of the buildings hang horizontally, rooted into the face of the quarry and suspended by magical forces.

Families live in the buildings and walk around in the rooms as they would any house ... the only difference being when they leave through the front door, they need a flight charm to stop them crashing to their death. There's a charm for everything in the S.P.M.A. and if you know the incantation, you can make a flower attach to your arm, spinning like a propellor to guide you safely to your destination.

As Society families go about their business, floating to and from their houses, Conrad and I stick to more traditional travel, walking through the busy region towards a place the weary and wise frequent: Poridian Parlour. It's a big, white building that's shaped like a palace, dominating the quarry

Each room draws a different crowd: one for tea and cake and another for the more competitive minded immersed in board games. The grandest room is for private gatherings, full of professors obsessing over formulas for new charms. Joseph is likely to be in the tea rooms, drawn to his mysterious contact once more, probably engaged in a game with the odds stacked against him.

We step through the busy entrance of Poridian Parlour, heading for the tea rooms and a potential duel with the evening witch.

4

UNFINISHED BUSINESS

We spot Joseph in the furthest corner of the tearooms, sitting with his back to us — reinforcing the sense he doesn't want to be seen. The busy room, decorated by tables full of tempting cakes, makes it hard to work out who his companion is, but I'm already sure it's Alice Aradel. Our Williynx maintain their tiny forms, fluttering through the air nearby.

As we ease our way past the crowded tables of witches and wizard, I spot the disfigured face keeping Joseph company. Disfigurement is a common trick used by Society members who want to go unnoticed. The combination of two Society remedies — Laudlum and Srynx Serum — causes purple veins to bulge in your neck and face, making you almost unrecognisable.

The disfigurement charm doesn't disguise Alice Aradel well enough, the evening witch sensing her chosen meeting point isn't as safe as she originally thought. Her thin, pale hands are a giveaway along with the heavy red lipstick she always wears. Thinner than I remember, she still emanates menace — the very vindictiveness that's caught a harmless wizard like Joseph in her web.

"It's her," Conrad whispers as we near, the glittering interior of our invisibility charm deactivated just at the right moment ... close enough to be in striking range whilst narrowing Alice Aradel's potential escape routes. She notices our presence too late, engrossed in whatever Joseph has brought for her to view ... magical artefacts probably unlikely to be of the harmless kind.

Whatever she's put Joseph up to is about to be revealed before an evening witch gets her comeuppance. The steel artefacts on the circular table are gathered up by Joseph at the sight of Alice Aradel's changing expression. He pulls his worn, black cloak tighter in a sign of unease, turning to face two familiar figures staring closing in on him.

"Morning, Joseph," Conrad offers, ensuring the blue fireballs swirling around his hands are in full view.

The eccentric wizard grips his leather satchel closer to his body, stuttering a nervous response. "Morning, Master Kusp. A pleasant surprise to bump into you."

Some older wizards keep up the 'Master' / 'Miss' greeting for some reason, probably their passive-aggressive way of hinting their dislike of under age members in the Society. *Tough* I say, because *these two* underage wizards saved their universe from destruction while they were scrambling for cover.

"You seemed in a bit of hurry this morning," I add, keeping Alice Aradel in my peripheral vision. She's clearly reaching for something in the pocket of her red coat. Hopefully, it's not a move to activate a charm — the one false move I need to render her powerless and on the way to a slime-covered cell in The Velynx.

"I ... I was in a hurry, Miss Grayling," Joseph offers in

reply, his thinning black hair and ripped black gown reminding me of how fragile he is. I keep this in mind as Conrad lifts his right hand in a warning shot to Alice Aradel.

"We were just wondering what your sudden interest in The Shallows is, Joseph?" I add, my all-black attire of leather trousers and cropped top designed to show the war wounds marking my arms and stomach — fine scars acting as a reminder of my skill in tracking down malevs. Alice Aradel knows this only too well, once siding with a wizard with designs on destruction: Erent Koll.

Koll and his army came up against a significant Society force, including thousands of sleeping soldiers, sky urchins and giants from Sad Souls. As well as endless magic, the S.P.M.A. has *might*, engaging Koll and his evil army to keep things on an even keel.

Since then, things have been fairly smooth in our secret universe, but there are always those drawn to the darker side of things and Alice Aradel is one of these people.

"I'll have whatever's in that satchel of yours, Joseph," I add with a glimmer of a smile. I don't like scaring people unnecessarily, particularly vulnerable wizards, but need to make the point that Night Rangers are *always present* ... *always* tracking those who start acting shiftily, reminding them of the consequences of betrayal.

"Of course, Miss Grayling," Joseph replies, nervously handing me his satchel. "Just common Society artefacts," he adds.

I already know this, but also know that some common artefacts have *uncommon* magical powers like a Zombul, for example -- the first thing I take out of the leather satchel. A Zombul is a small silver artefact with tiny holes puncturing the top: a defensive device allowing the release of any creature under your control.

A quick look inside tells me no real crime has been committed; it's just a simple trade with a witch skilled in the art of uneasy bargaining: a malev born with bad intentions. Alice Aradel is too weak and slow to overwhelm Conrad and me, which doesn't stop her trying. Removing her right hand from her pocket, the flash of her penchant stone signals an attack in the form of a blast of colour and light streaking towards Conrad.

Conrad is also marked by war ... far more conditioned for fire and fury than our weakened witch, uttering 'DISIRA' to extinguish Alice Aradel's fire before adding 'Fixilia' to add a different tone to things ... the sight of the evening witch grimacing at every movement causing Joseph to wring his hands in fear.

The eccentric wizard tries to back away from the mild carnage, almost falling off his chair and knocking over the petite woman bringing tea and cake to the table. I utter 'Magneia' to stop Joseph's fall, mildly amused when he pauses mid collapse, his chair hovering on two legs.

"Easy, Joseph," I say, putting the leather satchel over my shoulder. "We haven't got to the tea and cake yet."

With Joseph nodding in compliance, I deactivate the Magneia charm and help him back to the table. The Magneia charm is a simple magnetic force used to establish who's in control. Jacob knows who's in charge, and as Alice Aradel's disfigured face turns a shade of red I think she's getting the message too.

The petite waitress shuffles between the strange scene, keen to place the tea and cake on the table without getting caught up in our polite battle. As the waitress steps out of harm's way, returning to the counter, Conrad deactivates the

Fixilia charm and reaches for a cake from the silver tray, popping it into his mouth in one go.

"You can lose the disguise now," he says to Alice Aradel who glares in our direction, rubbing the back of her neck strained in a failed attempt to escape capture. When you've battled with colossal, fire-breathing beasts, vampiric birds and invisible, mind-bending monsters, an ageing witch is the least of your worries.

The only thing left to do now is join Conrad at the table, piling into the cakes and reaching for the tea. After all, a girl's got to eat. We sit together like this for a few minutes, taking in the old-fashioned glamour of the tea rooms. The standout feature is the vaulted roof made of stained glass, the S.P.M.A. logo decorating the centre. It's cool, all right, and with the mild drama of the morning under control, we get to the question of judgement.

Conrad and I sit between Joseph and Alice Aradel, ensuring neither of them attempt any sly moves. We carry our power lightly, I think, squeezing out as much fun as we can as we roam through the streets and skies, checking on shady figures whose movements are tracked on surveillance devices.

There are different types of tracking devices, small and large. The most user-friendly one is a Follygrin: a small, circular, leather-bound notebook you can carry around in your pocket. It's the thing I used in the barber's chair, watching Joseph Flint jump through the air on carpets made of white weeds, towards the place we're sitting in now.

Panorilums are hidden in a normal-sized book, unfolding into a massive piece of parchment, allowing the user to track multiple people at once. The other surveillance device, and also the biggest, is a Tabulal, only found in The Orium where senior Society figures track gathering forces — forces with the potential to form war lines.

The Tabulals have been quiet in recent times, and our job is to keep it that way. With Conrad getting his fill of cake and tea, I turn my attention to Alice Aradel whose disguise is falling away. The purple veins bulging on her face fade, revealing the familiar vision underneath ... of a fallen witch without the tribe who once protected her, hoping for mercy from the girl she once tried to kidnap: a girl with a habit of holding a grudge.

"Long time no see, Alice," I begin, the two swords acting as my weapons resting on my lap. Joseph sits perfectly still alongside me, jolting every time I reach for more cake.

All work and no play isn't the life of a Night Ranger, so I stuff another cake in my mouth and think of the flight back to The Cendryll. We'll rise high into the sky once more ... Conrad by my side ... the boy with piercing green eyes and a taste for battle.

"Save the sarcasm, Grayling," the evening witch offers in reply — we never were close.

Referring to me as 'Grayling' gives her a false sense of superiority, but she lost that edge a long time ago. Even before I fought in war, she wasn't the sharpest witch or even the fiercest. Like all bullies, she targeted vulnerable wizards like Joseph who asks if it's okay to have the last cake, making me feel guilty for stretching out this intervention. Joseph is innocent of wrong doing beyond offering a few common artefacts to a bad egg.

Does he know Alice Aradel is still in hiding because of her association with a dark wizard? Does it matter? Not really because Aradel isn't on the wanted list, so it's more my issue than anyone else's. In a nutshell, her plot failed, leaving the S.P.M.A. to live on and her sort to hide in the shadows.

"You've aged," I say, sipping my tea whilst Conrad readies his counter move, sensing that Aradel might have one last trick up her sleeve.

"And you're still a child," she replies with a humourless smile. Her thin, gaunt face isn't improved by the heavy, red lipstick.

"A child tasked with flushing out bad eggs, like you."

"And taking them where, may I ask?" she prompts, looking up at the stained-glass roof as she does.

"The place for bad things and bad people," Conrad adds in indirect reference to The Velynx — a statement that causes Joseph to whimper in fear.

"I've survived this long in the wild," the evening witch states, rising out of her chair, "and I imagine I can survive a little longer." She reveals her last move, attempting to flick open a Zombul to release a flurry of fury, but Conrad is one step ahead of her, whispering 'Weveris' to form a flying web which smothers the blast of vampiric birds attempting to burst free.

The sudden screech sends a wave of panic through the tea rooms, wizards and witches standing in defensive positions as swathes of light and energy burst into view ... rising and circling towards the enemy force ... a force many are just realising is the evening witch herself.

With Conrad muting Alice Aradel's attack, the only option she has left is to flee, but the crowds have vacated their tables, merging their beams of multi-coloured light towards her, gesturing for Conrad, Joseph and I to step back from the table: an army of sleeping soldiers stepping into the fore once more.

"Not quite the morning I had in mind," comes the voice

of Elin Farraday: a kind, portly wizard related to a Society legend and friend.

I offer Elin a smile as I step back, realising my two swords won't be needed. "An old foe trying to slither her way back in."

"Well," says Elin as he whips his charm towards the trapped figure of Alice Aradel, "it looks like she'll be slithering her way to The Velynx. We can take it from here, Guppy."

With a nod, Conrad and I whistle for our Williynx to return to a more majestic form which they do with elegance and ease — a vision of turquoise and powder blue gliding through the arcs of light and energy which have brought a fallen witch to her knees.

"I take it Joseph requires no attention?" Elin asks as we climb onto our feathered companions.

I leave the reply to Conrad who, after glancing at me, replies, "He's fine. In the wrong place at the wrong time."

Elin and Joseph exchanged a knowing glance as our Williynx take to the air, rising towards the vaulted, stained-glass roof.

"Jysyn Juice on you this evening, Joseph," I say to ease the eccentric wizard's nerves. It's also a way of letting him know he's not entirely off the hook.

With the evening witch dealt with, my powder-blue companion blows out a flume of white air — air that turns the stained-glass roof to liquid moments before we blast out of sight.

5

A CHANGING CENDRYLL

We glide through the sky, the cold air of the winter morning rushing by. The evening witch will be restricted by various charms before being questioned. Based on what she's been up to, she'll either be released with a clear warning or escorted to The Velynx where a slimy cell awaits her.

I doubt she'll be there for long because her crimes don't extend beyond illegal black market trading, and the alleged kidnap plot of young wizards who are now immersed in Society life. Only a select few know about Alice Aradel's plan to kidnap us when the flames of war were at their highest.

Her dark deeds faded into insignificance when the dust settled, though, the collective trauma of hundreds dead, colossal creatures killed and a terrifying artefact dominating the memory.

Malevs ran for cover when wanted lists were compiled: the main figures on the list being the captors most loyal to Erent Koll. The people in question continue to hide in places like The Shallows, but the realms beyond The

Society Sphere are endless, and it would take an entire Society army to track them down.

The decision has been to rely on a loyal group of Night Rangers, leaving sleeping soldiers to recover from the trauma of war. Witches and wizards drawn to darkness always slither out of the shadows eventually, and when they do, I'll be ready to re-introduce myself. The sight of swirling snow tells us we're approaching The Winter Quarter — the hidden, magical part, at least — igniting Conrad's desire to equal the scores in the sky.

"I gave you a head start earlier," he says with a wry smile. "You know, always the gentleman."

Erivan, his turquoise Williynx, morphs into a larger form, spreading its wings in expectation of a sudden surge of speed, and I brush my brown hair away from my face in preparation for round two.

I *hate* losing and Conrad knows it, tapping his legs against his Williynx to kick start the second race of the morning, sneaking a head start to trigger my anger: the very thing he wants to ensure the race is as fiercely contested as possible.

I race through the sky on the back of Laieya, closing in on Conrad who instructs his Williynx to release a blast of feathers: a simple trick to limit my vision, but this is easily navigated, a simple drop and spinning motion below the cloud of feathers, bringing the snow-covered streets of The Winter Quarter into view.

Conrad puts his unique skill as a sky rider into action, wanting this moment to last as he enacts a sudden, vertical ascent, climbing ever higher until I struggle to maintain his direction of flight. Then he releases a white web courtesy of the Weveris charm ... a web that opens as it falls, leaving only one thing to do ... spin off the Williynx and fall towards it, knowing this is what Conrad had planned all along.

Unlike our fall towards the snow-covered streets, there's no shifty wizard to track and no mission to complete, so I let out a laugh as I fall, hearing Conrad's yelp of joy behind me as we hit the web at the same time, grabbing onto each other as it wraps itself around us. The Weveris charm has a multitude of powers .... often used against the enemy, but also able to morph into protective forms like the romantic blanket around us now, cocooning us from the snow as we fall.

"You smell good," I say as I hold on to Conrad, running my hand along the scar on his neck. He never likes me touching it, the scar reminding him of his dad's tragic death, but Theodore died a hero and, as I keep reminding the boy I love, heroes deserve to be remembered.

"You don't smell so bad yourself," he quips as we fall at exhilarating speed, the white web tightening as if it senses our need for intimacy.

With a kiss, I run my hand through Conrad's copper-blonde hair, the surge of warmth flooding through me as it always does. "So, ice or flight?" he asks in reference to how we're going to enter another familiar realm.

We've already been collected by our Williynx this morning, inches from the ground, so ice it is. The Weveris charm is deactivated, releasing us back into the open and the blasts of ice follow ... two perfect channels streaking towards us, swooping under us until we can plant our feet on them, allowing us to skate on ice.

We slide on the paths of ice at a descending angle until the rollercoaster of fun begins, a screech of joy from me as the ice paths swoop upwards, spinning us in loops as we climb ever higher ... towards the Perium in the sky and The

Hallowed Land in the grounds of The Cendryll ... where Jacob is introducing a legendary Society game to his impressionable students.

~

THE HALLOWED LAWN IS JACOB'S CHOSEN PLACE FOR LESSONS involving a degree of risk. With his class receiving their foundational training, Jacob's version of the curriculum has brought him to defensive charms. Although the Society has accepted the need for greater unity, the admission of underage members follows a strict protocol.

It wasn't as simple as: 'Hi, kids. Just to let you know we work in a secret, magical universe and you've been chosen to join!'

It took time, selection and surveillance to test loyalties. After all, most kids can't keep a secret for ten minutes let alone a lifetime, but a lifelong commitment is what's expected, meaning the weak willed and loose-tongued were rejected: the Removilis charm removing all memories of their time in the S.P.M.A.

It would be ridiculous for a secret, magical Society *not* to have a memory altering potion, and the Removilis charm is ours, leaving the kids who've talked their way out of selection none the wiser. In the end, the eight were chosen, giving my brother his first class. I tried to talk Jacob out of it, suggesting he'd be bored teaching magic instead of *using* it, but he's determined to forge a new path.

Jacob's been with me every step of the way, from my entrance into the S.P.M.A. to the brutal reality of war, and it's strange not to be with him now. Circumstances change, though, leading people to choose their own path. My brother's six foot tall and lean with shoulder-length hair: kind, patient and considerate, making him the perfect candidate for teaching.

The morning return to The Cendryll is to help Jacob introduce a game to his class, thinking he might need help in explaining the intricacies of *Rucklz*. A game requiring skill and wit, *Rucklz* originally formed part of the initial training for new witches and wizards, the theory being that if you couldn't handle theoretical battle, you weren't cut out for a real one.

A board game in its original form, *Rucklz* is popular among Society folk, including in the tea rooms of Poridian Parlour. Formed of a collection of dots, the aim of the game is to activate one of the dots, transforming it into an object of attack or defence, depending on the order of play. Jacob's idea is to create *Rucklz* on a much larger scale — out on The Hallowed Lawn which has become his training ground.

He's using the game to improve his students' reaction time. The class are improving their knowledge of defensive charms, Jacob says, but are still too slow in their response. *Rucklz* will simulate a friendly battle, forcing them to improve their intellectual and physical dexterity: two things needed when magic is called upon in sticky situations.

The Hallowed Lawn gets its name from generations of heroic witches and wizards who've given their lives for the continued protection of the S.P.M.A., Conrad's dad being one such legend. Their ashes get released here in the presence of every Society soldier, marking the earth forever with the memory of the dead.

Jacob's chosen this particular place for the space it offers and for its symbolic importance: a reminder of the consequences of misusing magic. He's also realised that a traditional classroom is too limiting for effective tutelage, so The Hallowed Lawn it is. The threat of 'returning to the classroom' is normally enough to keep The Fateful Eight under control: a group of students with an interesting mix of intellect, talent and a general sense of indestructibility.

I remember feeling that way once but life has a way of humbling you, offering sharp reminders of how fragile all things are: lessons the excited, young crew will learn in time. Conrad and I have been called in as reinforcements, helping to referee the game. *Rucklz* is a game that can get out of hand when hot headed characters are involved, and this is Jacob's first attempt at recreating the board game on a much larger scale, leaving me to wonder what chaos awaits us.

WE APPEAR IN THE SKY ABOVE THE HALLOWED LAWN ON OUR paths of ice which our Williynx continue to create for us ... a dramatic entrance causing the eight students to turn away from Jacob's tutelage, chasing the turquoise and powder-blue feathers floating towards them.

Whoever catches a feather first gets a ride on their chosen Williynx. I laugh as the path of ice beneath my feet surges towards the immaculate grass, allowing me to keep my balance as I tilt with the curves of ice. Conrad stays low as the lanes of ice guide us towards Jacob, our hair lifting in the crisp morning air as we touch down to the excited yelps of The Fateful Eight.

That class is made up of four boys and four girls: Ava Blin, Tom Koll, Kate Follygrin, Roan Khan, Tilly Flint, Olin Zucklewick, Leah Creswell and Ethan Lyell. Ava is the tallest of the group, something she's self-conscious about while Katie is the most competitive, and Tom the most sensitive. Tom's fully aware of the dark stain over his family name, created by an infamous wizard.

Tom's nothing like his great uncle but still feels the need to gain people's trust. Luckily, Ethan has become close friends with Tom, a boy with all the style and sensitivity of his great uncle: the legendary Weyen Lyell. Ethan continues the Lyell tradition of large afro hair, his athletic frame lending itself well to lessons centred around physical dexterity.

"Morning, lovebirds," Jacob says in welcome, offering me a brief hug before shaking Conrad's hand. He always gives Conrad a 'parental look' — a weird joke they share regarding our 'growing relationship'.

Luckily, I've avoided the awkwardness of 'boyfriend meeting parents' because my dad's never really been around and my mum ... well, let's just say she's 'finding her feet' after a dramatic downfall. Mum used to be a big fish in The Cendryll but now she spends her days on the margins of Society Square — in a house left to her by Kaira's grandad, but I'm getting off track: back to *Rucklz* and the magic of defensive charms.

"How're The Dream Team?" Conrad asks, unable to hide his amusement at Jacob's evident frustration.

"Annoying and over excitable," Jacob replies, the top button of his shirt undone with the Society tie hanging down. He didn't respond well to the idea of uniforms for teachers, relenting at the suggestion of a tie. His blue jeans, untucked shirt and jumper make up the rest of his 'uniform': a brother I miss on my adventures.

Leah Creswell yells in excitement as Conrad's Williynx takes off from The Hallowed Lawn, taking the student who caught the first feather on a trip through the skies. The rest of the class crowd around us, desperate to know about our recent adventures.

"Have you caught any malevs recently?" Ethan Lyell asks, patting his afro to maintain its perfect form.

"We've bumped into a few," I say with a smile.

"Can you teach us how to skate on ice in the sky later?" Tilly Flint asks, the most skittish of the group, giggling nervously after every statement. I find her a bit annoying, wanting to snap her into the reality of the life she's chosen.

The first question she'd asked us was what it felt like to battle Erent Koll. The question brought blushes to Tom Koll's face: the great nephew of a sinister wizard.

Tilly isn't the brightest but has a kind heart, leading her and Tom to become friends once he'd forgiven her thoughtless comment. With cliques forming among the students, it's time to find out who's going to make the grade. After all, their lessons will come to an end at the end of the year — the time when a decision will be made regarding their suitability for life as permanent witches and wizards.

The successful few will take their places in Society faculties or one of hundreds of shops spread throughout England. Here, they'll settle into a life between the above ground world and the secret, magical universe they've had the fortune to be selected for. Selection, though, is only the beginning.

Jacob's got his theories on where they'll all end up, certain that only four of them will want to range beyond the safety of The Society Sphere: Ethan Lyell (because of his natural gifts), Tom Koll (out of a need to prove himself), Katie Follygrin (due to her competitive spirit) and Olin Zucklewick (out of sheer restlessness).

Conrad thinks that Roan Khan is the dark horse: quiet and brooding as if he's planning his future but only time will tell. My money's on Tilly Flint whose scatty nature is partly an act: the perfect foil for a young witch seeking an advantage within a group who know what's at stake: a life of wonder or a return to above-ground drudgery.

"Time for a bit of carnage, I think," Conrad jokes.

Jacob claps his hands at this statement, getting the attention of his students. "Okay, class: time to master your defences."

"Defensive charms!" The group shout in joy only to be disappointed by a shake of the head from Jacob.

"Not quite. We'll look at defensive charms again this afternoon, but before we do that we need to check your reflexes and reaction times."

"Why?" queries Tom Koll.

"Because if you have to use magic, you'll want to be confident you can activate it at the right moment."

"Like when malevs show up?" Ava Blin asks, her eyes glinting at the thought.

"Right," Conrad states, "or to just be confident that any charm you need can be ignited at the right moment. Today's lesson will help with your speed and dexterity."

"Sounds boring," Katie Follygrin mutters.

"*Rucklz* isn't boring, I can assure you Katie," Jacob replies, struggling to hide his dislike of Katie's sullen, self-centred nature.

"*Rucklz...*?" Olin Zucklewick queries — the smallest of the group. "Isn't that boardgames?"

"Not the way we play it," I add with a sharp clap of the hands which makes the group jump. "If things go to plan, you'll either be running for your life, dragged to safety by our Williynx or smashing things into a million pieces, gaining you victory."

"*Wicked*," Ethan Lyell says, patting his immaculate afro

again, as if he's preening himself for an end-of-game interview.

Katie eyes Ethan who's always her first choice for a teammate, mainly because she's got a secret crush on him.

"Well, what are we waiting for?" Katie asks impatiently.

"For the Williynx to blast a streak of ice into the sky," Conrad explains, gesturing towards our turquoise and powder blue companions, hovering above the young wizards.

"Time to choose the teams," Jacob states, taking out his Vaspyl and throwing it into the air, transforming it into a whistle. "Any moaning and you'll be sent inside with a mark against your name. Time for the games to begin."

6

A HELPING HAND

Jacob adjusts his tie before saying, "Remember, everything you do goes towards your final mark, and our final decisions. It's pass or fail: our magical world or the boring one you sometimes have to return to. *How* you play this game is as important as winning."

"*What*?" Katie queries.

Ignoring Kate's disgruntled comment, Jacob blows on his hands and releases a flurry of Quij: the luminous, colourful insects that light up The Cendryll. "You're all familiar with the board game *Rucklz*, but we're creating our own version of it out here."

With that, he gives us the nod to introduce light to the occasion, the utterance of 'Canvia' releasing streaks of light and energy from our hands: topaz blue from Jacob and I while Conrad's hands turn the colour of tanzanite. Without further explanation, we go to work marking out the outer boundaries of the game.

"While Conrad and Guppy prepare the pitch for you," Jacob continues, having his class' full attention now, "go over the charms we've been learning: the Bildin charm particularly. Obviously, *Rucklz* is based on your ability to *build* which is where the Bildin charm comes into play. Be imaginative and *fast*, remembering not to fall into the traps your opponents set."

"Like what?" Roan Khan asks as he loosens his tie.

"Like masking steel in a glass shell," I add, "or losing your temper and forgetting to defend before you attack. *Rucklz* is about holding your nerve and managing your mood. When you lose your temper, you lose control, leaving the objects you make to expand out of control, dragging you up into the air or across The Hallowed Lawn which is when things get messy."

"So, it's *dangerous*?" Leah Creswell asks, still exhilarated from her brief trip in the sky on the back of Conrad's Williynx.

"We're here to make sure it's safe," Conrad explains with a reassuring smile, "which doesn't mean you go all guns blazing. *Everything counts,* remember: every lesson, every improvement and every mistake, so get ready."

Conrad and I complete the pitch, stepping between the blue and tanzanite dots framed within an enormous square ... the Quij hovering above the boundary of the pitch. Moving into their hoped-for teams, the young wizards wait to be put into teams.

"Someone's going to end up in the air," Conrad whispers as Jacob organises the class into two groups.

"Yep," I nod, already knowing that the most competitive are going to fall short, making self-centred decisions that will undermine their team's chances.

"Ava, Katie, Roan, Olin: Team One," Jacob calls out, a cloud of anger passing across his face the moment Katie challenges his choice. "Tilly, Ethan, Tom, Leah: Team Two.

Take your positions on the boundary and wait for my call. Guppy and Conrad are going to demonstrate the rules of Rucklz before we begin."

"First, we need team names," I say as Conrad joins me in the middle of The Hallowed Lawn. "Captains, step onto the dot closest to you."

After a bit of murmuring and cajoling, Katie and Ethan step forwards.

"Right," Conrad says to the captains. "Team names"

A quick discussion returns "Wicked Wizards" from Ethan's team and "Slick Sorcerers" from Katie's.

"Okay," Conrad adds, whistling for his Williynx to take up position above Ethan's team.

I do the same, gesturing for Laieya to rise into the air on the opposite side.

"On Jacob's call, each person steps onto a dot," Conrad continues. "You are *not* allowed to move from your dot until you've created your shape of attack or defence. You create your shape by tapping the dot *like this* and imagining the shape you want; it will form in your hands less than a second later.

Remember, Jacob's chosen *Rucklz* to improve your *reaction time* when using defensive charms. We're looking for *this specifically* so whether you win or lose isn't as important."

Stern nods follow from each team, fragile friendships replaced with intense stares as their desire to secure their place in the S.P.M.A. intensifies.

"One of the benefits of being out here," I add, "is that the shape you create can *grow*. You use your arms to create the width you want and your imagination for the height. *But* if you lose control of your shape, you'll be dragged off the pitch and out of the game. *Rucklz* is a game of *subtleties* ...

knowing when to strike and when to counter strike, setting traps for your opponents until they've got no point of attack or defence: *like this.*"

Conrad and I touch the dots we stand on, generating two vast shapes to demonstrate the majesty and might of *Rucklz.* Conrad's chosen a line of daggers — glittering tanzanite weapons which hover momentarily before flying towards me. I'm ready with a block of steel which halts the daggers' velocity, the steel wrapping itself around the daggers before it lifts, re-forming into a wrecking ball that swings towards Conrad's head.

Ethan's team scrambles for cover as the wrecking ball crashes onto The Hallowed Land, rolling towards Conrad who uses the flight charm to propel himself into the air, touching the dot he lands on to create a vast crevice that the wrecking ball sinks into. With the wrecking ball contained, he throws out a spinning orb that whizzes towards me, and I react with a handful of dynamite which detonates the orb, sending shards of light spinning in the morning air.

We step off the playing field with a smile and a hug, letting the shards of light fade before Jacob claps his hands to jolt his stunned class to attention. "So, that's *Rucklz,*" he says with a smile. "Any questions?"

The students are too stunned for questions, realising their limited training might not be enough for this version of *Rucklz.* With a second clap of his hands, the Williynx release a shower of feathers, leaving Conrad and me to form crests for each team: a gladiator crest for Ethan's 'Wicked Wizards', and a Merlin crest for Katie's 'Slick Sorcerers'.

With the stage set, stadium lit and team crests created, we take our positions on the side lines, ready to referee a match likely to have its fair share of drama.

THE GAME BEGINS WITH THE SOUND OF JACOB'S WHISTLE. Ethan's team is faster out of the blocks, taking their positions in a triangle formation on their part of the pitch. It's an interesting strategy, helping them to activate their dots and thrust out a variety of objects before Katie's team can orient themselves.

Ethan punches the air in delight as the ball bearings he's formed bounce towards the opposition ... Roan and Ava managing to jump at the right moment whilst Olin mistimes his jump, landing on two of the ball bearings and falling flat on his face.

"Get up!" Katie yells, her competitive spirit already spinning out of control as she launches a spear at Leah - the girl she's competing with for Ethan's affections.

Leah forms a shield with ease, crossing Tom's path to fling it back in Katie's direction. The shield is formed of Mithium — indestructible steel — so there's no danger of it shattering when the spear makes contact. With their defences intact and the team moving with greater agility and speed, Ethan's 'Wicked Wizards' close in on Olin who's struggling to get to his feet.

Olin finds his bearings just in time, creating a steel cage around himself as a shower of bullets rain down, bouncing off his cage as he yells in frustration. With Ava and Roan gaining in confidence, partly in the knowledge that no spear or bullet can penetrate their steel wall. The action intensifies as Katie roars her team forwards, jumping into the air as she throws a spinning arc of steel towards Ethan and Tom who are now working in tandem.

They smash away the arc of steel with their swords before their weapons transform into a bow and arrow, releasing a flurry of arrows towards Katie who slips as she forms two shields: a mistake that ends her participation in the game as the arrows thud into the shields, knocking one of them out of her hand.

"One nil!" Ethan shouts as his teammates roar in delight.

With Katie out of the action, screaming her frustration from the side lines, Olin comes into his own, spinning low as weapons fly his way. Jacob, Conrad and I keep the Magneia charm activated, ensuring no weapons make contact with the students: a simple charm which draws objects towards us when they're in danger of striking the students.

I draw a scythe-like object to me, manipulating its trajectory to make sure it whizzes past Ava's head. After all, I doubt anymore parents will be sending their kids to magic school if a student ends up in hospital!

Sensing the need to force home their advantage, Ethan's team split into two pairs with Tilly and Tom taking on Ava and Roan ... leaving Ethan and Leah to target Olin's small form. They've fallen into a trap they don't see, though, Olin pretending to lose his footing again as Katie screams at him from the side lines.

It's a clever trap, appreciated from our referring position on the west boundary. Olin has pretended to slip to draw his opponents closer, dropping onto his stomach as spinning orbs fly towards him, missing him by inches. Seconds later, he strikes out with fireworks that he's buried in the ground — camouflaged by a simple use of the Invisilis charm: the obvious advantage no other student's thought of.

As Ethan and Leah close in, Olin releases the fireworks, wrapping himself in a steel cylindric shield as they crackle and explode through the air ... darting towards Ethan and Leah's shocked figures who scramble to form their defences.

They're a second too late and the half-formed swords are splintered, disintegrating seconds later and sending to the side lines.

A roar from Laieya and Erivan signals another shift in the game, reaching its climax with the least likely candidates left standing. Team One are now led by Olin: the diminutive, dark haired wizard with a gift for silent strikes. He calls Ava and Roan towards him, quickly organising a triad formation reminiscent of the ones used in my own battles.

Every witch and wizard has a particular gift, normally discovered in times of trouble, and it's fair to say Olin's discovering his on The Hallowed Lawn: a boy with a gift for cunning attacks. If I was to put my money on anyone becoming a Society soldier, it would be the least likely of the class: Olin Zucklewick — grandson of Ivo Zucklewick who runs the Society bookshop in Founders' Quad.

Olin shouts orders to Ava and Roan as a blizzard of objects bounce off their pyramid shield: a defensive wall that suddenly blasts open with the trio riding in the air on the steel walls. The three sections of the shield have become a floating army, taking their opposition by surprise. Ethan's two remaining team members — Tilly and Tom — duck as Odin, Ava and Roan release an additional shower of steel in the form of creatures crashing onto The Hallowed Lawn.

I'm a little taken aback by the creation — a feeling shared by Tilly and Tom who get caught in two minds regarding the necessary defence. They decide on webs to trap the creatures before changing their minds at the last minute, producing a steel mesh instead.

The mesh wall doesn't form in time, bringing a collective cry of 'DISIRA' from us: the disintegration charm obliterating the steel creatures seconds before they descend on Tilly and Tom.

Team One, led by Olin, have won the first game of *Rucklz*, something the ever-confident Ethan and Katie find a little unnerving. As self-assured as they are, each has fallen short in today's test, making them realise their future in the S.P.M.A. isn't going to be plain sailing, after all.

7

FAMILIAR VISIONS

With The Hallowed Lawn returned to its immaculate state via the use of a Repellia charm, Jacob sends the class off to lunch — a signal for the students to activate portable Periums, transporting them back to The Cendryll. If they're anything like I was, they'll take a detour to Founders' Quad, heading for Wimples sweet shop or Merrymopes milkshake and ice cream parlour.

They're under *strict* orders to stay within the boundaries of Founders' Quad, either returning to their rooms in The Cendryll or enjoying the Society shops in the above ground section. Not that this will stop them exploring. I wasn't one for rules myself which got me into a *world* of trouble: the sort of trouble Jacob is keen to protect his students from.

There's no evil force to worry about, meaning Jacob has an hour to relax. He's a little more serious than he used to be: the consequence of being responsible for eight students, I suppose.

I've tried my hardest to talk him out of committing to a career teaching new witches and wizards, but he remains committed to a quieter life. It's only Conrad and I who can't resist the pull of The Society Sphere — the endless realms offering a mixture of wonder and freedom. Although we're still young, we're as equipped as any witch or wizard, allowing us the freedom of discovery.

With the final student disappearing through their Perium, Jacob, Conrad and I put the finishing touches to The Hallowed Lawn, ensuring the divots are ironed out and every blade of grass is replaced. It's a sacred place, after all, and although the Society elders aren't precious about the use of the ground, its maintenance is another thing altogether.

The sky clouds over suddenly, leaving us to activate our own portable Perium: a curtain of light leading us into temporary darkness. Once inside, we walk through a tunnel of doors, each one getting smaller until we arrive in the Cendryll.

The Cendryll's where everything started, leading me to the life I live now. It's also a reminder of the infinite power magic offers — the beautiful, delicate Quij fluttering in the air, carrying books to and from the bookcases perched under the vast skylight.

The big change is the presence of sky urchins and giants from Sad Souls. Not everyone's got used to having sky urchins around the place, some of the more nervous members jumping every time the scar-ravaged creatures approach. It probably doesn't help that they've refused to change their black rags for something more 'fitting' as Elin Farraday likes to put it.

Abandoning their uniform would be an abandonment of their traditions as a species conditioned for war, they argue, war which has given them their scars. They move through The Cendryll crowds proudly, taking the more nervous members of Jacob's class under their wing: a symbol of one marginalised group recognising another.

Everything's about unity now so no one dares make any group feel uncomfortable, leaving the ageing giants to lend their services to the creation of charms. The giants are called Ulux. They lived in a grey, depressing place called Sad Souls for *years* until the elders got a grip and realised the groups they most relied on in times of need deserved greater recognition — a recognition that started with *inclusion*.

"We should go and say hello," Jacob suggests as Casper and Philomeena Renn appear on the spiral staircase: the two adults who took us under their wing in uncertain times.

Jacob's *big* on loyalty, regularly reminding me of the need to show my face around here more. I know he's right because The Cendryll is home now — the only home I've ever really known. Helping Jacob out with his students is my way of showing my appreciation — to a brother and a magical faculty — but life as a Night Ranger means perpetual motion, so I'll be off again soon, seeking new adventures and putting a lid on trouble.

Thankfully, Conrad feels the same, travelling with me on my journeys throughout the S.P.M.A., including the 'alone time' we always manage to fit in. Let's face it, the Society can be *demanding* and there's no better example of that than Kaira's dad and aunt: two legends who have sacrificed so much.

So, it's time to do some quick hellos, checking in on familiar faces, before I'm off through the skylight on the back of my powder-blue Williynx, hoping I'll be able to avoid Jacob's questions about mum.

"Keeping out of trouble, Guppy?" Casper Renn asks with

a smile — ever the elegant leader dressed in a light-blue suit with matching shirt and tie.

"Mainly," I reply, returning the smile and nodding to Kerevenn: the first giant I ever laid eyes on. Kerevenn's all angles and bones but has a gentle nature, helping to take the edges off the sky urchins' blunt interactions with more timid Society members.

"And are we fitting in time for romance?" Philomeena Renn asks, her good looks and flawless brown skin always reminding me of Kaira.

I don't ask about Kaira, partly because it always makes me sad to think of her journeying through the S.P.M.A. on her own, but also because I know her dad and aunt miss her as much as I do. Instead, we skirt around the issue, discussing the progress of Jacob's class.

"They're pretty *fierce*," Conrad states.

"Who's your money on?" Casper asks, regarding those likely to make the grade.

"Ethan, Ava and Olin at the moment," Conrad replies, looking up at the Quij who flutter above our heads, their bodies glowing a warm orange in welcome.

"Olin definitely," I add. "He's the dark horse of the group, playing the fumbling wizard to his advantage."

"So, bumped into any shifty characters lately?" Philomeena asks, dressed in a slick, all-grey trouser suit.

She knows we have, but is really asking about our decision to let Joseph Flint off the hook.

"Just the evening witch."

"Alice Aradel?"

I nod. "Trying to get her hands on some artefacts: Zombuls mainly."

"What did she have over Joseph to get him to sneak

them to her?" Casper asks, sharing his sister's elegance and flawless, brown skin.

"That's what we're going to find out later," Conrad replies, clearly eager to get back into the morning air.

Like his Williynx, Conrad isn't designed to live a magical existence cooped up inside a faculty; he's born to roam, seeking thrills to feed his taste for adventure. I'm also keen to leave before the 'mum' question comes up, something Jacob picks up on.

"Have you seen mum lately?" he asks already knowing the answer.

I avoid his gaze, glancing at Laieya who licks her powder-blue feathers near Quandary Corner: the quiet seating area I once claimed as my own. "I'll go soon."

"She's on her own, Guppy."

"I know."

"Are you ever going to forgive her?"

"What she did isn't easy to forgive."

"You promised you'd try," Jacob adds, tapping me on the arm to get my focus. "Let old wounds heal, Guppy."

I let my brother's comment resonate for a while before I repeat my promise to visit mum ... in the twisted building on the margins of Society Square. I clearly *haven't* let old wounds heal because the building reminds me of *why* she's forced to live an isolated existence. Mum was at the heart of The Cendryll until she made *a massive* mistake during a particularly heartless phase.

She *wasn't* there for us and treated us like an annoyance she'd rather be rid of ... happy when Kaira's dad and aunt took us under their wing ... so why should I feel the need to visit her...? Don't parents have to *earn* their children's respect...?

Anyway, enough of that — time to get back to the skies

and a few more tight squeezes with Conrad, just in case you thought being a Night Ranger was *all* about tracking down shifty witches and wizards.

"Why don't you go and pay mum a visit now?" Jacob pushes, giving me *the* look.

"Maybe tomorrow."

"It's always 'tomorrow,' Guppy. Do it for me — one more favour before you go gallivanting off."

Conrad steps closer, placing an arm on my waist as a signal of support. He knows how uncomfortable I am in my mum's presence, but he's lost both his parents and hasn't got a brother's love, so I give in. "*Okay*. We'll go now."

"Say hello from me and tell mum I'll be over this evening."

I give Jacob a smile — the brother who always puts others before himself. He essentially brought me up, protecting me in my more *spontaneous* days in the S.P.M.A. He's a reminder of the love surrounding me, something I sometimes forget when I'm wrapped in Conrad's arms. Family, after all, is forever.

~

WE SAY OUR GOODBYES, EXITING THE CENDRYLL IN THE traditional manner, choosing a rickety door behind The Seating Station where Society elders discuss day-to-day events. There's less drama these days but they still *love* debating the benefit of certain charms, or whether teaching a group of under-age wizards will turn out to be a good thing.

Conrad and I leave them to their debate, pulling the brass door handle out and turning it until The Hallowed Lawn appears in gold lettering. With the door handle pushed back in, we step through the door and find ourselves back in the open air — our Williynx fluttering close by, shape shifting into their majestic forms as they rise up into the sky.

With Laieya and Erivan enjoying their own race in the morning air, Conrad senses my mood changing, realising it's linked to my mum. He takes my hand as we walk across The Hallowed Lawn, the feeling of the light rain falling onto my skin. I'm not a big hand holder usually and Conrad knows this, only offering this gesture when introspection threatens to get in the way of our adventures.

"It will get easier over time," he says, offering me *that smile*.

"It hasn't got easier so far."

"You've never made it easy on your mum."

"Why should I?"

"I'm not saying you should, Guppy, but if you punish her forever it's never going to be easy."

I turn to Conrad, pushing my body into his as I kiss him: a kiss I let linger until he runs his hand through my brown hair, his surprising strength an unspoken symbol of his need for intimacy. He has no family aside from me now — the Society his only home — and I'm forced to remember this as we continue to kiss: a Fire Witch whose fury won't allow her to forgive.

As thunder sounds overhead, I let out a light laugh — my way of accepting I'm wrong about my mum. I *do* need to forgive in order to move on and, most importantly, not turn into the bitter person she's become. It goes without saying how dangerous anger can be when you throw magic into the mix.

"Come on," Conrad urges as the rain lashes down. "Let's get to your mum's before we get drenched."

I sneak another kiss, wondering if we should just stay here as Conrad's jeans and T-shirt get soaked, his grey overcoat doing little to protect him from the rain. He's a *perfect specimen,* that's for sure, encouraging me more towards the idea of staying put.

Then again, Jacob's class will be returning from their lunch break soon, and I imagine he won't want them stumbling across us: a Fire Witch and a sky rider making the most of the rain.

8

THE TOUCH OF LOVE

The twisted building mum lives in is hidden within a wall of protective charms. Although everything's peaceful in the Society, mum made a *lot* of enemies when she was a senior member of The Cendryll: a position of power that went to her head.

To cut a long story short, the last war was centred around a hunt for a lethal artefact most people believed to be a myth ... that was until it turned out it really did exist ... and I'm sure you can guess what happened next.

Anyone harbouring dark desires crept out of the woodwork: malevs, captors and The Prince of the Underworld — Erent Koll. They mainly ended up dead or banished, and my mum got the 'rehabilitation treatment' in Sad Souls for trying to align herself to Erent Koll. *Now* can you see why I'm not desperate to visit?

That's how we know the ageing giant, Kerevenn, who's settled in The Cendryll now. Kerevenn was the giant who oversaw my mum's rehabilitation in Sad Souls. I'm sure you're wondering how my mum got away with rehabilitation when others were banished to The Velynx: the faculty for bad things and bad people.

Well, luckily for her, Casper and Philomeena Renn had already taken Jacob and me under their wing, meaning if they stuck my mum in The Velynx we'd be parentless. Also, she didn't actually use dark magic — the one unforgivable sin in the Society — meaning she hadn't completely crossed the line. So, that's why she's stuck away beyond The Society Sphere, no longer at the heart of our magical universe. Anyway, time to say hello.

As our Williynx release a single feather, floating towards the roof of the twisted building, I hold firm in the promise I made to Jacob: to learn to forgive. We descend lower as the turquoise and powder-blue feathers make contact with the roof, turning it into the colours of the feathers to mark our arrival.

The light goes on in the bedroom window, signalling that my mother's not yet out of bed: a woman with little to look forward to. We touch down outside the front door, understanding the need for a gentler arrival, and I prepare myself for a visit I've been avoiding with Jacob's words echoing in my mind.

"I WASN'T EXPECTING VISITORS," MUM SAYS, PEERING OUT from behind the door.

She's still in her dressing gown, the once-perfect blonde hair a bit of a mess. After an awkward silence, she ushers us in and I use some Oomph powder to light the fire. Rehabilitated witches and wizards are banned from using magic, meaning mum's limited to a mundane life: an ex witch sitting alone with only her regret for company.

"I'll make some tea," Conrad says to break the silence, and I sit by the fire with mum, searching for comfortable conversation.

"How's everyone in The Cendryll?" she asks, still clearly missing the place.

"Fine. Jacob's turning into a good teacher. He's always had it in him, having to guide me growing up."

I grimace at my stupid mistake, catching Conrad's eye in the kitchen who gestures for me to move past it. Referring to Jacob as my substitute parent isn't going to help move things forwards, and as I'm on a mission of forgiveness I change the subject. "Jacob's coming round later; he said to let you know."

"That's good," mum adds, studying the fire as if she relies on it for company. "He always brings flowers."

She's broken ... a powerless figure who was a few steps away from ending up in The Velynx. I'm not sure living here alone is much better, but she's still got her family around her — not that I've played the dutiful daughter role very well.

"It's Jacob's birthday soon. I hope you can make it," mum says, keeping her eyes on the fire as if I'm somewhere else in the room.

I turn my attention away from her, looking out of the window into the darkness, studying the waves of defensive and protective charms swarming around the twisted building. As much as it protects her, it traps her too, and I know there isn't much I can do about it. "I'll be here," I say, forcing myself to utter the words. It will be the first birthday party I've attended since mum's demise.

We never celebrated birthdays growing up, something I still struggle with, but harbouring grudges is what I'm fighting against so I stand and help Conrad with the tea, wishing I could feel more for a mother whose compassion is buried deep inside her.

Like our visit to The Cendryll, I'm aiming to keep this brief, keen to avoid an extended stay and aware that we've got a date with Joseph Flint in The Chattering Tap. We got him out of a possible arrest in The Shallows which doesn't mean he's got off scot-free. He's still got to explain the reason he got involved with Alice Aradel in the first place, starting with how they got in contact.

"You look happy," mum says, offering a sad smile to Conrad and me perched on the armchair by the fire.

I wish I could change things for her, but I can't. She made an irreversible error of judgement so all I can do now is continue to search for the compassion she never had. I'm not the little girl who needs her approval anymore, understanding the scar her cold detachment has left.

I've got Conrad and Jacob to heal those wounds, I remind myself, sipping the tea and letting the silence linger, ready to return to The Winter Quarter and an eccentric wizard who had a lucky escape this morning.

~

I SAY MY GOODBYES WITH A GENTLE KISS ON MY MUM'S forehead, promising to return for Jacob's twenty-first birthday in a few weeks. We also say goodbye to Laieya and Erivan for a while, remembering that creatures and humans exits on an equal footing. Our feathered friends have their own places to roam, temporarily free of the duty we have chosen to burden ourselves with.

With Laieya and Erivan squawking a temporary farewell, we make our way to the small study by the narrow door in a corner of the room. Going through the standard ritual of pulling the brass door handle outwards, we squeeze through and shut it behind us, occupying an all-glass room.

From here, we can study all buildings in each of the quarters making up The Society Sphere: The Winter Quarter, The Gothic Quarter, The Hollow Quarter and The Singing Quarter. This used to be Isiah Renn's house, after all, the once-infamous wizard who turned out to be the Society's saviour. During Isiah's time as a wanted man, this room of glass served him well, providing a bird's-eye view onto every aspect of the Society: ideal for a man in hiding.

Each part of the room of glass moves, the floors becoming walls and the walls becoming ceilings, bringing on a feeling of dizziness as I try to zone in on the image of The Chattering Tap. Conrad handles the moving walls and floors better than I do, probably because he's more used to spinning and free falling with his Williynx.

The image of The Chattering Tap appears beneath our feet, Conrad tracking the moving floor as it becomes a wall. He taps the pane of glass framing the desired location, causing the image to separate from the glass structure, stretching as it floats down and wraps itself around us. All that's left to do is to reach out through the image as if we're piercing a fine layer of Society life.

We're inside the busy pub seconds later, stepping between two tables as we make our way to the crowded bar. I keep an eye out for Joseph Flint: a wizard who owes us a round of Jysyn Juice. We find Joseph in his usual position, sitting at the bar surrounded by a rowdy crowd who are trying to get Lorina Lellant's attention: the girl with a crush on Conrad. Joseph spots us as we approach the bar, offering a forced smile.

He knows he's about to be questioned on his secret meetings with Alice Aradel, and he's clearly on edge about it. At least he's not trying to sneak out again, like he did earlier this morning. That *would* make him look suspicious which wouldn't bode well for him. I push my way through the impatient group of twenty-something Society members, returning Lorina Lellant's glare. She can pine after Conrad all she wants; he's mine.

"Miss Grayling, Master Kusp," Joseph Flint offers as we sit on either side of him at the bar.

"Oi!" comes an annoyed grunt from the tallest of the twenty-somethings shoving into us: crude wizards with an attitude problem. "They're *our seats*, little girl."

The comment brings a hush to the pub — an acknowledgement of a mistake made. At the risk of sounding big headed, Eli Blin should have done his homework: a thin, oily specimen. His limited brain cells and sense of entitlement make him ignorant to Society history, including my skill in battle.

He's already had two warnings about his attitude, the last one linked to his secret taunting of one of the men in his group: Adam Creswell. Adam's got a stammer which the rest of the group endlessly tease him about. They're not his friends, but Adam's chosen safety in numbers as a survival tactic: a boy who isn't cut out for Society life.

"I said they're *our seats,* little girl, so unless you ... "

Eli doesn't get to finish his sentence ... a small object floating towards his head, making him lose his balance ... his skinny frame leaning one way then the other to the delight of the pub. It's fair to say Eli isn't a popular character, and the slow clapping starts, signalling the start of mild combat.

Eli's bravest comrade reaches for something in his pocket, only to have his hand wrapped around his neck courtesy of the Weveris charm: a simple web to end his involvement. With Eli still struggling to regain his balance, I step closer to him, ducking as he swings at me.

"You little *upstart*," he spits as he swings again, failing to make contact. "Get the Ozzer *off* me!" he demands, still under the illusion he's got any control over the situation.

An Ozzer is the artefact I've used to put him in his place: an object you throw in the air to destabilise your enemy. Eli is more an annoyance than an enemy although he needs to improve his manners, and I'm *just* the teacher to guide him.

"You didn't say *please*, Eli."

He swings again, this time with a lot more force, and I decide to swing back with a handful of Oomph powder — the yellow substance used to ignite an empty fireplace bringing a painful scream from him.

"All you've got to do is find your manners, Eli," I add as the crowded pub continues to clap, enjoying the duel.

He's in no fit state to fight back because he's a second-grade wizard, granted entry into the S.P.M.A. by the skin of his teeth. If anyone's marked for a dark path, it's Eli. His whole *energy* is wrong: a feeling I get every time I meet him.

"Okay, *please*," he finally relents and I deactivate the Ozzer, knowing this isn't the end of it.

As he whips out his arm, attempting to send the Promesiun charm my way, I spin into a Disira charm, vanishing from sight before reappearing behind him, framed by fire. He jumps back in shock as I move towards him ... the protective bubble of the Velinis charm protecting me from the fire's flames.

The design of my defensive charms means Eli's focused

on the flames, seeming to surging out my body: an image that brings silence to The Chattering Tap.

"The Fire Witch," Adam whispers as Eli's cowardly crew cower at the bar, grabbing onto Joseph Flint as if he's going to come to their aid.

The penny finally drops for Eli: the recognition that *the little girl* he ordered away from him knows what *real danger* is, and he isn't it.

"*Okay*," shouts Conrad, clapping his hands to break up the minor drama. "Back to your Society beverages."

He ignites a Spintz charm to get my attention, sending a shower of light above me to snap me out of a burgeoning fury. "That's *enough*, Guppy. We're on Society business, remember."

Accepting Eli's fear as a recognition of his error, I deactivate the Velinis and Smekelin charms, letting the flames fade around me. He's lost for words: the thin, oily bully who's unlikely to forget who I am.

"By the way," I say to Eli in way of conclusion. "Adam's a good friend of mine. Yeah, he's got a stammer but you've just been embarrassed by a *little girl*, as you like to put it. So, here's my advice: if you don't want to find out what fire *feels* like, look after Adam or I'll *take care of you*."

Eli glances at his cowardly group nervously, his oily, black hair adding to his shady energy. "Fair enough," he finally says, gesturing for his allies to head for the exit — a slow, sarcastic clap following the group out.

Adam Creswell glances back at me, hovering at the back of the group. He doesn't belong with them but has chosen intimidation over isolation, wondering why a girl he barely knows has helped him.

"*Beauty and unity*," I whisper, remembering a time when a sinister group of wizards bullied me. I had Kaira's dad and aunt to protect me, so I'll be Adam's secret guardian until he finds his confidence and proper place in the Society.

"*Ready now?*" Conrad asks, handing me my glass of Jysyn Juice: a non-alcoholic Society remedy. I return to my seat, raising my glass to Joseph Flint who forces another nervous smile, wondering how his day is going to end.

9

SOCIETY MATTERS

With Eli Blin taken care of, the focus turns to Joseph's secret visit to The Shallows. If he was a lover of Society board games like *Rucklz*, his trips there would make sense, but he's an eccentric who obsesses over Society facts. The one fact he should be clear on is the consequences of suspicious behaviour.

He sips his Jysyn Juice slowly, the courage infused within it the very remedy he needs. He'll be fine if he just tells us the truth — not so fine if he's thinking of concocting a story to cover his tracks.

"So," I begin, swinging my legs on the barstool, "What gives, Joseph?"

The tremor in his right hand worsens — the consequence of a charm backfiring on him in the testing phase. Joseph works in the Feleecian, the faculty for remedies, where powder of various colours fills the air. Williynx are more plentiful in the Feleecian, using their noses to assess the quality of new remedies. If they squawk, we're onto something but if they pass out we're not.

I found this process cruel at first until Jacob explained it was perfectly harmless. No Williynx is harmed in any way and the Society gets to catalogue new remedies: remedies used to benefit the S.P.M.A. and the above-ground world, adding a touch of magic to all things.

Obviously, non-magical people have no idea that the sweets in Wimples are laced with magic. The adults are bamboozled by the moving illustrations that form on the tongue, and their children don't care — the *wonder* of it all enough to bring them back again and again.

"Just my usual jaunt to The Shallows," Joseph finally replies, placing the glass of green liquid in his lap.

"I wouldn't say usual," Conrad adds as the annoying presence of Lorena Lellant hovers at our end of the bar.

"Drinks, lovely?" she asks, focusing on Conrad.

"We're fine, thanks," he replies, keeping his back to her.

She's all hair and smiles until that point, grabbing the empty glasses and shouting "Who's waiting" as she walks away.

"I ... I've been frequenting The Shallows more regularly recently."

"Indeed you have, Joseph," I add, wondering if the tremor in his right hand's got anything to do with my little fire display a few minutes ago. "The question is why the sudden interest...?"

"I received a request."

"From Alice Aradel...?"

Joseph nods, lowering his gaze in a gesture of contrition. "It's quite *empty* beyond Poridian Parlour, Miss Grayling, mainly frequented by those down on their luck."

"Caught out, you mean," Conrad adds, correcting the nervous wizard. "The evening witch was hiding out in The Shallows because of the choices she made."

His stained black cloak rests on the floor, collecting

more dust, reminding me of a professor lost in thought. "It was only a few artefacts," he states in a particularly unconvincing manner.

"Zombuls have a specific purpose," Conrad continues, gulping down his Jysyn Juice and slamming the glass on the bar, making Joseph jump. "Which makes me wonder: what would an evening witch like Alice Aradel want with a Zombul...?"

"She said it would help to keep her entertained," Joseph explains.

This brings a look of disbelief from Conrad and me.

"I bet it would," I say, standing from the bar stool, "and I doubt she was planning to use a Zombul to release harmless creatures like the Quij."

"The Society allows the trading of artefacts between its members, Miss Grayling, even those choosing self-exile."

"True, but I also know you're wise enough to judge a person's intent. On that basis, do you really believe Alice Aradel intends no harm with a handful of Zombuls in her possession?"

"That thought did cross my mind, Miss Grayling, but then she hasn't been charged with any crime."

"*Come on*, Joseph," Conrad says, looking a little annoyed. "You know she was in Erent Koll's pocket, and her band of malevs were the ones trying to kidnap us. We got you out of an awkward situation earlier, but playing dumb to the possible implications of your behaviour makes me wonder what you're hiding."

"Hiding...?" Mutters Joseph, struggling to mask his fear before adding, "Alice has a way of getting what she wants ..."

"Yes," I add, "by holding things over people: things they'd rather be kept secret. So, the question is, does your secret put you in the same bracket as Aradel and her mob ...?"

"*No*, Miss Grayling. She ... I ... She has a *reputation* which still sends tremors through less courageous wizards. It's the suggestion of what she might do, should her request be denied."

The tremor in his hand gets worse all of sudden: a sign we need to back off before the shaking turns into a stroke. I'm all too familiar with Alice Aradel's subtle threats and manipulation — the very tactics employed in Society Square to dominate black market trading until Society eyes turned on her, keen to question her loyalties. The evening witch thought better of attending an interrogation, deciding exile was the safer option.

"Easy, Joseph," I say, placing a calming hand on his shoulder. "If it's easier, just give us an idea of what Alice *really* wanted the Zombuls for. Her time in The Velynx will force the rest out of her, unless she wants it to be her new home."

Most prisoners would rather risk crossing Quibbs Causeway than remain locked up in a faculty laced with dark magic ... *The Velynx* words no witch or wizard wants to hear in relation to their questionable behaviour.

"I imagine she's looking to buy protection in The Shallows," Joseph offers, "her disguise suggesting she's exposed out there."

His hands continue to shake, signalling the need to ease up on the questioning. The little knowledge we've gained suggests the evening witch is looking for a new mob to surround herself with, the original cast splintering once the tide turned against them.

"Well," I say, placing my empty glass on the counter, "I'd choose my trades more wisely if I were you, Joseph. Luckily, it was us tracking you this morning; other Night Rangers might have had you arrested on suspicion of conspiring with an old foe."

The last statement seems to tip him over the edge ... a spasm causing his right arm to fly into the air, releasing the empty glass which smashes against the wall ... the green liquid landing on Lorena Lellant who screams in fury. All is forgiven, I decide, watching Joseph jump up from his stool, enacting a Disira charm to make a quick exit, keen to avoid another grilling.

I struggle to suppress a bout of laughter, watching as Conrad's superfan storms behind the bar, slamming the tray of glasses by the half-asleep sky urchin before she vanishes behind the red, baize curtain. It's turning out to be an entertaining morning.

"That was dramatic," Conrad declares, wiping spots of green liquid off his face.

"The beginnings of a new charm," I suggest, still laughing. "Just when you're cornered, you fling out your arm with the object in it, the randomness of it catching the enemy by surprise."

"We'd need a name for it," Conrad adds.

"The *Splat Attack*," I offer.

Conrad looks unimpressed. "Doesn't sound very *magical.*"

"*Rapid Splat*"

"Isn't that a kids' game?" he asks, drawing more laughter.

With our morning duties now complete, we have the rest of the day to ourselves.

"I think the Jysyn Juice has gone to my head," Conrad jokes, holding onto the bar for support as he feigns drunkenness.

I take him by the arm, indulging his attempt at comedy

as we head for the exit. "Don't worry, handsome, you've got the rest of the day to sleep it off."

That smile returns. "I can think of ways to stay awake ..."

WITH THE MORNING TAKEN CARE OF — MAINLY ENTWINED ON the top floor of The Weary Winzer — we prepare for our night shift: the main duty of all Night Rangers. This morning's journey tracking Joseph Flint was more of an intervention, ensuring good wizards don't fall into the traps the marginalised few set for them.

You can't rid a world of evil entirely, but ignoring it is even more dangerous — something the Society learnt the hard way — so the aim is to track and contain, neutralising potential problems as they arise: Alice Aradel a case in point.

With most parts of the S.P.M.A. running smoothly, night shifts often turn out to be jaunts to favourite realms. There are so many amazing places to choose from, making it hard to have favourites, although The Singing Quarter is my favourite part of The Society Sphere.

Like The Winter Quarter, it operates in two parallel worlds: an unremarkable above-ground one and a more spectacular space. It's the same process throughout the thousands of buildings making up our secret world: turning a brass door handle anti-clockwise once it's pulled outwards, waiting for your chosen realm to appear.

It took me a while to venture into all four realms within The Society Sphere: Founders' Quad and Society Square being my regular stomping ground until drastic events drew me beyond its boundaries, learning how to fight without the protection of my penchant: a Quivven helping with that.

Less Society drama means more fun, like morning flights and romantic trysts.

The evenings are for exploration of new places ... my aim to visit every place in the S.P.M.A. before I'm eighteen. This might sound ridiculous because I'm only sixteen, but not every realm can be accessed by just stepping through doors: some of them require specific procedures and pathways to access.

Gilweean is one of these places — where the Williynx originate from — and Sad Souls is another: the land of the ageing giants known as Ulux. Just trying to keep track of the names makes you realise how rich and complex this world of wonders is: a world I've got no intention of ever leaving.

~

WITH THE EVENING LIGHT FADING, I SIT ON THE WINDOWSILL on the top floor of The Weary Winzer, situated in Society Square. The shops are closing as the light fades, signalling the beginning of our night duties. Evenings are usually full of entertainment, the two Night Rangers we roam with — Noah Khan and Lucy Flint — always looking for the most interesting way to pass the time.

As Society Square hums to a settled rhythm, I turn to Conrad who puts on his grey coat. We made the most of our 'alone time' tucked away on the top floor of The Weary Winzer: a Society shop that sells perfumes, scents and pick-me-ups. The shop's popular with above-ground shoppers, hoping to find the scent of something to get them through the day.

It's surprising how tired non-magical people look, shuffling into shops like The Weary Winzer, snapping out of their glazed state at the sight of all the bottles lining the shelves ... bottles of different coloured liquids that give off a hypnotic scent.

Like all shops in the S.P.M.A., everything on sale is laced with magic — our way of giving back, you could say. I look down over Society Square from my high vantage point, watching a family of four step into The Weary Winzer, the bedraggled mum struggling with fatigue with her youngest child in full tantrum mode.

Parents arrive in certain shops in droves, the magical sweets in Wimples for example, keeping the children entertained for hours. There's something for everyone in the two main shopping sections accessible to the above-ground world — Society Square and Founders' Quad — shops that offer a little touch of magic to make boring lives more bearable.

Conrad appears beside me, rubbing my lower back as he follows my gaze onto the streets below. It's strange to think we were once part of the crowds, knowing nothing about the secret Society operating in plain sight. You would *never* guess and that's the beauty of it, I suppose, a seamless integration into normal life to avoid suspicion.

That's why Society members dress in normal clothes above ground, running all of our shops, making sure a link is maintained between the two worlds. After all, it would only take a few mistakes to create suspicion. This point is driven home by eccentric wizards like Joseph Flint who acts like he's from a different *planet*, let alone a secret Society hidden behind magical doors.

It wouldn't take many Joseph Flints for the uninitiated to start asking questions so dual living is encouraged, offering the ability to move between worlds.

"Where do you think Noah and Lucy will want to go

tonight?" Conrad asks, checking to see that we've left no trace of our time on the top floor of The Weary Winzer.

It's one of the many places we use to get away from it all, rarely used by the shop owners who smile each time a Williynx feather floats past the shop window: a signal that privacy is required.

"Noah will want to go to The Singing Quarter," I reply, adjusting my black leather trousers.

"If only he could sing."

"I think it's more to do with pining than singing."

"Still chasing Zoe Tallis," Conrad comments.

"Yep," I say with a smile.

"So, he's going to sing for her again?"

"He isn't *that* bad."

"He *clears rooms*, Guppy. It's *really bad*. I think someone should tell him."

"He's *your* best friend; *you* tell him ... or we could sing along with him. You know, show him how it's done. In fact, I can feel a song coming on now," I say, offering a few operatic notes, causing Conrad to head for the closest door. "Maybe a bit of karaoke if everything's quiet tonight...?" I tease.

"*No karaoke*," comes the reply as he waits for me by the door, ready to transport us to our meeting point.

10

NIGHT RANGERS

We meet Noah and Lucy in the Society section of Pat's Caff, situated in Founders' Quad. I like coming back here because it reminds me of my first adventures above-ground, sneaking into Tallis & Crake to upgrade boring artefacts for cooler ones before heading to Merrymopes for a Belly Blitz: the best milkshake in existence.

Merrymopes also has the benefit of The Revolving Room, the spinning structure that Jacob's students will need at some point, allowing them to move safely to allocated parts of Society Square.

We walk through the emptying streets of Founders' Quad, past Helping Hand — the shop for those down on their luck. A massive, ornamental hand moves up and down outside the shop. Once inside, you take your slip of paper and step into your allocated cubicle where your items are presented to you via a spinning mirror.

Like most Society buildings, Helping Hand has a dual purpose, the private Society cubicles providing access to Sad Souls: the land of the Ulux, better known as ageing giants.

Some Ulux have integrated into the S.P.M.A. while others choose to stay in Sad Souls, not quite ready to cross the threshold into mainstream magical living.

Pat's Caff sits in darkness, the 'Closed' sign shimmering on the shop door — a little touch of magic to illuminate the darkness. The side entrance is where we're headed, accessible to the initiated. I buzz in the code on the brass plate, feeling my silver penchant bracelet vibrate as the red door opens, leading into a narrow hallway found in similar buildings.

Once the door closes, the rug in the hallway rises inches off the floor ... hovering vertically in the air ... the pattern beginning to fade as we step closer.

"Entrinias," I say, uttering the charm to access certain secure areas.

The pattern on the rug fades completely, replaced by clearer visions of what lies beyond, only the outline of the rug remaining. Steel seating pods fill the space we step into, and I hear Noah's loud laughter before we spot him, holding court in the highest pod located nearest the ceiling.

The pods are made of an indestructible steel called Mithium, a multi-coloured force field of energy suspending them in mid-air. A Spintz charm gets Noah and Lucy's attention, the shower of light signalling our arrival. They place their penchant rings on the edge of the steel pod, lowering it towards us.

As the steel pod reaches us, I nod to the gathering of Night Rangers who often meet here before their shift begins. Being a Society soldier can be demanding so finding ways to let off steam is helpful: the laughter coming from the pods a sign that all is well.

"Quick," Noah urges, "We've got a bet going. Taeia thinks The Ameedis are a fiercer creature than the Mantzils, but I keep telling him the Mantzils *smash minds*. He's willing to bet a *thousand Kyals. Tell me* you've got a Zombul on you, Guppy?"

I nod, patting the pocket of my leather trousers.

"*Brilliant*!" Noah adds excitedly as Lucy rolls her eyes.

"Thank God you've arrived," she says with a weary smile: her pixie looks and slight frame masking a fierce spirit. "Noah's been driving me mad with his need to win."

They'd make a nice couple but Noah's only got eyes for Zoe Tallis who, I'm sure, will be mentioned soon when he tries to drag us to The Singing Quarter. There's no plan to use the Zombul to test Taeia's flawed theory; the Mantzils' mind-splitting cry would unhinge most minds present, but the threat of it will probably be enough to shut him up.

"A *thousand* Kyals," Noah repeats, his pot belly always seeming at odds with his skinny frame.

He started in the Society at the same time as Jacob, training with my brother before things started to *explode*. Luckily, Kaira's aunt came to the rescue, getting them to help her in creative charms — the lucky break they needed, using the education to master charms.

Noah's always the loudest person in the room, clapping his hands in excitement as we rise towards Taeia's group of Night Rangers: an athletic lot who are fiercely competitive. Taeia likes the look of himself. He's undeniably good looking and knows it although his arrogance is more than a little off putting.

He's inherited the good looks and flawless, mixed-race skin of the Renn clan, but without the elegance or unique gifts of the Renns *I* know: Kaira, Casper and Philomeena. Kaira never mentioned Taeia but, then again, she barely knew her extended family when I first met her. Taeia's nothing like Kaira: all brawn and brute force as if he's trying to prove he's worthy of the Renn name.

"The Fire Witch to the rescue," Taeia comments as our steel pod returns to its position near the ceiling.

His surface confidence hides a deeper insecurity ... the reason he's got himself entangled in a bet for a thousand Kyals: Society money. Kyals come in handy when you want to trade artefacts in Tallis & Crake.

"The Terminator as predictable as ever," I reply, returning the sarcasm, confident I'd have the better of him in battle. He's brash and arrogant, brandishing his Night Ranger status like a badge of honour and making enemies in the process.

"So, you crossed Quibbs Causeway without a scratch, Grayling?"

He calls everyone by their last name, thinking it gives him some sort of edge. We'll see how that works out for him. I do my best to ignore him, signalling hello to the more friendly Night Rangers occupying nearby pods.

"And you handled the Mantzils with ease...? Their screams didn't unhinge you?"

"Mantzils, Ameedis, Viadek, Dexametris," I say, continuing to look away, knowing how much it'll annoy him. "All monsters have weaknesses at the end of the day."

"As easy as that," Taeia comments bitterly, leaving Conrad to put him in his place.

"If it was easy, we wouldn't have the scars, but if you still think the Ameedis is a more dangerous creature, let's find out with a Zombul. Noah and Lucy can unleash each creature and we'll see who's left standing."

The fragile confidence falters at the idea of facing the monsters in the flesh ... not that Conrad's going to do anything of the sort, knowing that releasing underworld creatures outside of secure training facilities is strictly forbidden.

"No worries," Taeia states, throwing a bag of Kyals towards Noah. "It was just a friendly bet to pass the time."

A brief silence falls until Noah breaks into laughter, partly shocked by full payment of the bet, but also concerned at the look in Conrad's eyes — as if he's about to release a deadly creature anyway just to put Taeia in his place.

"Time for the night shift," I state, tapping Conrad on the arm.

We're a Society at peace, after all, letting grudges pass, having learnt how quickly they can turn into bitter feuds.

THE DIVISION OF SOCIETY DUTIES FOLLOWS THE SAME pattern, an informal agreement for the gathered Night Rangers to cover the various realms beyond The Society Sphere. We're returning to The Shallows to investigate Alice Aradel's need for protection. A lack of conflict doesn't mean a lack of drama, and I wonder what drama's about to unfold in The Shallows.

"So, *Alice Aradel* appears out of nowhere, trying to get Joseph Flint in her clutches," Noah says as our steel pod makes its descent.

"What excuse did Joseph give?" Lucy asks, adjusting the belt on her jeans.

"That the evening witch was buying the Zombuls for protection," Conrad replies. "Weirdly, the excuse seemed genuine as unlikely as that sounds."

"Was Alice her usual charming self?" Noah adds as each group of Night Rangers lines up by the door we entered Pat's

Caff through. I'm about to return to the barber's chair I sat in earlier — the unique Perium offering access to The Shallows. Many realms don't need this security but the Shallows remains a strange place, balancing oddity with a strange energy, and where there's uncertainty, additional precautions are put in place.

Joseph Flint's words have got me thinking ... *what if*. What if he's telling the truth and the evening witch is running scared of an unidentified group, calling on an eccentric wizard's sympathy?

Joseph is as loyal as they come so, like Conrad, I'm inclined to believe there's an *element* of truth to the story, meaning if Joseph *is* telling the truth, we've got a target to track down. We might be a Society at peace, but there's rarely a dull day in *this* magical wonderland.

THE FAMILIAR ROOM IN BANNERIN'S BARBER'S RE-APPEARS AS the side door to Pat's Caff re-opens: the private room housing a particular Perium. We make quick work of sitting in a barber's chair, staring through the peephole as the chair edges closer to the wall. The peephole expands seconds later and we're sucked through gently.

No staircase appears this time — an oddity of this particular portal — and we find ourselves in the land of floating carpets again. It's my second visit to The Shallows today, ready to use the Magneia charm to call a carpet of weeds to me again. As I wait for my floating form of travel, I take my trusted Vaspyl from the pocket of my leather trousers: morphing steel ready to be shaped into any weapon I need.

With the soil twisting and turning in every direction, I glance towards Noah and Lucy on my right and Conrad on my left: a loyal crew on another night mission. There won't be any help from the skies, Society creatures enjoying the peace of Society faculties or attending to other realms.

The S.P.M.A. footprints in the soil remind me of the strange nature of The Shallows: a place where your penchant offers little protection. The Society Sphere is the point at which your penchant's protective power fades — a Quivven used in its place. A Quivven is a small, brass hexagonal object buried under the skin.

I don't expect any surprises, relying on the fire charm surrounding me as I kneel on the floating carpet of weeds which picks up pace as we near our destination. As we approach the quarry housing The Shallows, the buildings bursting out in every direction light the way. The horizontal and upside-down buildings are always striking at night — like unique lighthouses guiding travellers to safety.

There isn't much of a threat out here at the moment, but that could all change if Alice Aradel *really was* trying to buy protection. I imagine she'll reveal all unless she wants to stay cooped up in The Velynx: not a place *any* witch or wizard chooses to step foot in.

If the evening witch is telling the truth, she'll be released; if not, it will be a quiet evening's work. Poridian Parlour comes into view, my fire charm signalling the night's surveillance has begun ... on the trail of possible malevs in the making.

~

EVERYTHING IS AS EXPECTED INSIDE, THE HANDFUL OF SOCIETY members who lodge in Poridian Parlour resting in leather chairs, studying intricate moves on board games or trying to stay awake: hardly a threatening bunch. This changes soon after we've taken our place in The Grand Room, keeping our distance from two Society elders in heated debate.

"The Domitus," Noah whispers at the sight of two figures entering through the sliding doors ... a man and a woman with emotionless expressions ... sitting at the table closest to the door.

"Since when do they come to Poridian Parlour?" Conrad poses, holding the gaze of the bearded man staring over at us.

They are the group authorised to track and tame dangerous creatures: an honour given to a select few. Riadek are the creatures being tracked and tamed at the moment — better known as Silverbacks. They're huge, winged creatures with steel armour that can do *serious damage.* The Silverbacks are ferocious creatures once under the control of evil forces, meaning I don't trust them *or* The Domitus who tame them.

The Orium Circle has a different view, though, and since they decide the laws there's no point dwelling on it. In their view, taming dangerous creatures is better than killing them without cause: a plan that might backfire if another powerful witch or wizard goes rogue.

"Is it me or are they staring at us?" Lucy asks, whispering 'Promesiun' as flickers of citrine light form around her hands: a defensive charm, just in case.

"Maybe they're annoyed we interrupted their little deal with Alice," I add, offering a sarcastic smile to the female figure who looks like she's in need of a shower — the greasy hair and dirty fingernails doing nothing for her appearance. I've met this kind before: a detached breed, enjoying the power they wield.

They end up being harmless robots who carry out their duty of protecting the Society or, more rarely, gifted witches and wizards with dark dreams of dominance. I'm not sure where these two fit in but one thing's for certain, they haven't dropped by to play a game of *Rucklz.*

"I think they're here for us," Conrad says, uttering 'Comeuppance' to ready his Vaspyl for transformation: morphing steel for malevs in waiting.

The silent pair probably aren't dangerous but nothing's left to chance these days, so I call over the tired waiter and order a round of Jysyn Juice. It's a Society remedy designed to provide courage to the more nervous in our circle. Courage isn't required but patience is, so I flip the Vaspyl in my hand, waiting for the two Domitus to make their move.

"We can't have a staring contest *all night*," Lucy says, her impatience getting the better of her. "The Domitus are famous for their silence so let's break it — go over and say hello."

"Why?" Noah queries, wishing this was already over so he can persuade us to head to his favourite part of The Society Sphere, continuing his endless pursuit of Zoe Tallis.

"To find out if we need to track them or move on."

"I say move on," Noah replies with a wink and a smile — an obvious attempt to abandon the cause. "If they were bad eggs, we'd know about it by now."

"We didn't know about my mum until it was almost too late," I counter, holding Noah's gaze to shut him up. He's being distracted by romantic leanings and as much as I get that, we've got a job to do. "We *wait* until they leave or make their move, whatever that's going to be."

"It might just be them flexing their muscles," Conrad suggests, tapping my arm in a gesture of pause. He's worried I'm spoiling for a fight which I'm not, but I *do* want answers so we can establish the truth of Alice Aradel's supposed fears.

"Well, if we're going to have a staring contest I think we're going to need cake," Noah says, rubbing his pot belly.

"You *can't* still be hungry," Lucy comments, the faint flames of the Promesiun charm decorating her hands.

Patting his belly, Noah adds, "It's the night shift blues ... always gets me."

"Then don't do them."

"But then I wouldn't see *your lovely mug*."

Lucy shakes her head, deciding to return her attention to the static pair who look upwards at nothing in particular, as if they've got a seventh sense to the creatures moving in The Society Sphere. It adds to the enigma they're clearly working hard to maintain: a pathetic waste of energy if you ask me.

At the end of the day, we're all warriors fighting for the same cause. Well, that's the theory, at least.

11

SHIFTING WINDS

As the rooms in Poridian Parlour begin to empty, Noah focuses on the cake as we sit out the first part of the evening, maintaining our silent stand-off with the emotionless pair. It's difficult to judge whether they're just miserable gits passing the time, or if there's more to it.

I shake my head when offered the final slice of cake — Noah and Conrad having demolished the rest — focusing my attention on the mood of the pair. If taking out a Nivrium wasn't such an obvious move, I'd retrieve one from my Keepeasy and place it on the table. A glass of water poured into the water reader would activate the three silver lines, giving us more of a clue to the intentions of the emotionless pair.

Jacob's right when he says I can be paranoid but, then again, I was right on the first day I met Kaira, sitting in Quandary Corner and watching adults come-and-go in the middle of the night. They, of course, weren't paying attention to me sat alone on the ground floor of The Cendryll, not doing a very good job of disguising their movements.

That little dance led to all sorts of madness, including being chased by Melackin and tracking a mysterious lady in white. The lady staring over at me isn't dressed in white, silver-grey garments covering her body, and she isn't trying to hide anything — but the lack of communication between the two of them has its own mystery, as if they want to stand out.

"Odin Blin," whispers Noah through a mouthful of cake.

I can see why he's got the pot belly now, being averse to anything nutritious.

"Who's the lucky girl?" I ask, gesturing towards the static lady with the dead eyes.

"Neve Blin," Lucy adds, stirring her tea with a silver spoon. "They're not the sort of people you see around here, normally stuck out in Drandok taming Silverbacks."

"A miserable place for miserable people," Conrad adds, getting impatient with the status quo. "Look, we either go over and say something or move on. There's no law against sitting in silence and staring at people — maybe that's their thing."

"I say we introduce ourselves," I suggest.

"You would," Noah comments, never one to want to ruffle feathers. "Let's just get out of here and have some fun. Isn't that the point of *being* a Night Ranger? The ability to go wherever you want, when you want."

"I'm with Guppy and Conrad," Lucy adds, deactivating the Promesiun charm as she stands, indicating no desire for conflict.

As she does this, the pair of Domitus stand from the table near the entrance, flicking a glimmer of light into the air ... light courtesy of the Spintz charm ... a signal for something waiting outside.

"The Silverbacks," I whisper. "Got to be. They've come to flex their muscles."

"*Silverbacks out here*?" Noah queries, suddenly losing his appetite.

"Probably," Conrad adds. "Ego and attitude; I've seen it all before. They're obviously allowed to ride tame Silverbacks beyond Drandok: a little power play. Boring, if you ask me. Come on, let's go and roam somewhere with a bit more fun."

The sudden shudder causes us to pause, studying the pair as they make their exit towards whatever's waiting for them outside. It's the Riadek: Silverbacks with an attitude. I mean, what else makes that kind of racket in the middle of the night?

The old me would want to follow them to check out their training ground in Drandok, but that's not my role now, maturity having mellowed me at some point. Instead, we head over to the window, catching sight of Odin and Neve Blin as the expected creatures descend from the sky, their huge wing span only rivalled by the Williynx.

If there was ever a statement of intent, this is it, risking bringing their Silverbacks into a busy realm beyond The Society Sphere. It isn't illegal but it *definitely* isn't encouraged, and I don't like the statement; I don't like it at all.

As Odin and Neve Blin climb onto their Silverbacks, they glance up at the window we're stationed at: a strange smile touching Neve's mouth.

"I *told* you it was for us," I state. "They want something from us."

"Like what?" Noah asks.

"Like a duel in the sky to test who's boss," Conrad suggests, rubbing his fingers together: a sign he's plotting something.

"Well, we've got the best sky rider in the S.P.M.A.," Lucy says, watching the figures as they roar through the sky, disappearing seconds later. "If they want a duel, let's give them one."

"A duel with *Silverbacks*?" Noah queries, suddenly looking a little pale.

On the surface, it looks like a strong breeze would blow him over, but his anxiety turns to measured fury when he's tested. His quirky dress sense also gives the impression of a mild mannered wizard, but he's far from it if you get on the wrong side of him. Chinos, T-shirts and waistcoats are his current look, never bothering with a coat unless the temperature falls below zero.

"If they want a duel, they can have one," Conrad states with a look of defiance.

Like me, he hates bullies and never backs down when faced with one. Odin and Neve are either bullies or have a fiercely competitive spirit, and there's nothing wrong with the latter. In fact, the more I think about it, the more a duel in the sky between Silverbacks and Williynx sounds like fun.

A gladiator battle without the killing. We've got remedies for minor injuries and can easily organise referees to oversee the friendly rivalry — the friendly part being a loose term. The Silverbacks have armour as a weapon and the Williynx have ice: ice that killed The Prince of the Underworld so I know who my money's on.

"Right, we're out of cake and talking about crazy duels," Noah says, watching the Silverbacks rise into the evening sky. "I say we get out of here before we agree on something I'm going to regret."

"Not The Singing Quarter unless you agree to the duel," Conrad says with a mischievous smile.

He knows how much Noah loves to be the centre of the attention, and The Singing Quarter is always full of life, humming until the early morning hours: a welcome break from Night Ranging.

"I'm in," Lucy says, nudging Noah as she walks past. "*Come on*, Sinatra. Clear your lungs and find your courage. You never know, mentioning the duel might get Zoe's attention."

That perks Noah up — the thought of Zoe Tallis finally going on a date with him.

"Only if I get to sing three songs and you sing along with me."

Conrad heads for the door at this request, realising he's been out manoeuvred.

"Did I hear a 'yes' from the sky-rider of the century?"

Noah doesn't get a yes, so it remains to be seen if Conrad's willing to risk public ridicule to put The Domitus in their place.

~

THE SINGING QUARTER IS SITUATED ON THE SOUTH SIDE OF The Society Sphere. It's the most boisterous of the four quarters, drawing high-spirited witches and wizards who like to shake off their Society duties with remedies and revelry. It's hilarious to walk through a shop in the above ground section, maintaining its hum drum tones, before stepping through a Perium into a hidden world of magic and revelry.

It got its name from a group of wizards who refused to stop singing until a law on opening hours changed. Apparently, the Society elders were more uptight in the past, thinking there should be a curfew on fun. The singing wizards got their way, mainly because they started singing between worlds, belting out their tunes above ground: a sight that brought unwanted attention to them.

The tipping point was when the police arrived in Merrymopes, the famous milkshake and ice cream parlour, responding to complaints from above-ground residents. The singing wizards ran upstairs when they spotted the police, pretending to be terrified but knowing they were heading to a Perium on the top floor.

Apparently, the two policemen waited for over an hour, insisting they come out, finally getting the key for the door only to find the room empty. *DRUNKEN ASSAILANTS EVADE CAPTURE* was the headline in the above-ground papers, leading to a reconsideration of the law on opening times in popular drinking establishments.

The Singing Quarter isn't decorated by perpetual snow like The Winter Quarter; its magic is more subtle. We appear by Rebel's Rest with Conrad still mulling over Noah's deal: a duet for a duel. I leave him to make up his own mind, knowing how embarrassed he gets at the thought of public displays.

"I bet any money he backs out of the deal," Noah whispers as we turn down the alleyway leading to Rebel's Rest.

"A thousand Kyals?" I say, offering to relieve him of the money he won from Taeia in Pat's Caff.

"A *thousand*? I thought we were friends?"

"Sorry, I thought you were confident."

"Have you *even got* a thousand Kyals?"

"I can get my hands on it."

"I bet money he doesn't," Lucy counters in reference to Conrad refusing the duet for a duel deal.

I could tell Lucy a few things but she's weird about personal stuff.

"Okay, the bet's on. A thousand Kyals a piece," Noah states with confidence, moments before Conrad bursts into song — a sight that even shocks me.

The three of us watch Conrad do a 'Singing in the Rain' rendition, swinging around a lamp post as he activates a Spintz charm, sending showers of light above him, manipulating them so they fall like raindrops around him.

"Is he *drunk*?" Lucy asks, mouth open at the sight.

The strangest part is that Conrad can *sing,* bellowing out the notes in the most surprising event of the evening. Noah's lost his bet and needs to focus on reaching Conrad's heights: the thought of a duel with The Domitus hanging over him.

I click my fingers for him to hand over the bag of Kyals — Society money — pocketing it in my Keepeasy stitched into the pocket of my leather trousers. Keepeasies make things disappear until you need them again, and I'm already thinking what artefact I can get my hands on with the money. It's not a case of needing things but it's *fun* to barter for things on the Trading Lane in Tallis & Crake.

Noah grudgingly agrees to deliver Lucy's thousand Kyals in the morning, reverting to his habitual sulk on facing losses. He's a *terrible* loser but needs to get over himself if he's going to woo Zoe Tallis with talk of a duel in the sky. With the bet decided and the noise reverberating from Rebel's Rest, Conrad ends his spontaneous musical rendition, returning to my side.

"You never do that for me," I tease, taking his hand as we head towards the entrance, looking forward to an evening of remedy and revelry.

"I've been waiting for the right moment," he says with *that* smile.

"Maybe you can do it again later."

"I'll see how the throat feels," he adds, putting his arm

around my waist: the boy with more secret talents than I know what to do with.

"So, should I drop the 'duel' thing in before or after my songs?" Noah asks, rubbing his hands in preparation.

I want to say 'before' because he can't sing to save his life, but as he's lost the bet I go easy on him, eventually suggesting, "afterwards".

"Work your magic first," Lucy suggests, finding the whole obsession with Zoe Tallis ridiculous. "Then by the time you get to the duel, she'll be eating out of your hand."

"Or begging for mercy," Conrad adds, darting through the door before Noah can grab him.

A roar goes up as we enter, mainly from the group of friends we've formed here: not Night Rangers but faculty-based members who think sleep is a waste of time.

"The Singing Magician!" Jalem shouts from the back of the strangely named 'rest rooms'.

The group pounce on Noah, ruffling his floppy dark hair out of affection. They're *pure fun* with no hidden agenda, keen to hear of our exploits throughout The Society Sphere, but equally keen to have a good time: an ideal reminder to enjoy the universe of wonders we somehow found our way into.

"What's the song?" Harvey asks, handing us glasses of Liqin — a remedy designed to remove hallucinations but also effective at relaxing the mind: non-alcoholic of course.

"I'm not sure," Noah says, following Jalem's lead, downing the first glass of Liqin. "Conrad's just done a version of *Singing in the Rain*."

The jovial group pause in puzzlement, turning their attention to Conrad who's easing away into the corner.

"No *way*," says Ilina. "Conrad *sings?*"

"Like an angel," Noah offers grudgingly.

"*Duet*!" comes the expected cry: a request Conrad's ready for, knowing the pain of performance will get him his duel with The Domitus.

"*One* song," he says, looking on edge, "then I've kept my side of the bargain."

"What bargain?" Jalem asks, a friend most easily described as all bones and angles.

"A duet for a duel," I say.

"A duel? With who?"

"The Domitus."

And with that, the rest rooms fall silent.

12

DUETS & DUELS

Ilina breaks the silence as concerned gazes rest on us, mainly from Society elders who've got a habit of shaking their heads when young wizards are mentioned. There's not a lot of head shaking at the moment — more expressions of annoyance at the rumour of a duel amongst comrades.

"Who's authorised a duel?" Ilina questions, maintaining her Gothic look complete with flowers in her hair.

I wonder if she thinks she's in a film, surrounded by a group of adoring men who do everything to protect her. Not that she's a damsel in distress or anything; she just gives off that vibe. Ilina can hold her own in any crowd, her sharp wit putting many of her peers in their place. She's wise, too, meaning the look on her face suggests she thinks the duel is a bad idea.

"No one's authorised it," Conrad replies, sipping the Liqin in the knowledge the rumours are going to spread, meaning our Scribberals will be rattling when we return to The Cendryll.

Scribberals are the communication device used in the Society. It's a silver box with a small handle. You write your message and place it into the box. Once the lid is closed, you swipe the handle on the side and *whoosh* — the message vanishes, appearing in the Scribberal belonging to the person you're writing to seconds later.

"No one *will* authorise it," Jalem adds, stooping to avoid the lampshade above his head. "It's the sort of thing that starts rivalries, and we all know where *they* lead."

"Relax, Jalem," Conrad states as he gulps down the Liqin. "It's just a bit of competition: one sky rider to another."

"I doubt The Orium Circle will see it that way," Harvey adds, the opposite of Jalem with trousers that burst at the waist.

Noah might have a pot belly but Harvey has an overall roundness: 'genetics' he likes to say. "No one's going to allow you to duel with the Riadek. They *rip through flesh*."

"Not the tame ones," I add, taking Harvey's glass as a prompt to drink faster. "Anyway, I think we should check out how tame they are first with a little trip to Drandok. If all looks well, we'll see if Odin and Neve want what they seem to be looking for: a way of finding out who masters the skies."

"Conrad, obviously," adds Ilina, adjusting the flowers in her hair. Unlike a lot of the girls my age, she isn't flirtatious around Conrad which isn't to say she doesn't like him. There's liking and *having*, though.

"Maybe I am and maybe I'm not," Conrad comments in reference to him being the best sky rider, "but it'll be a good test. It's also a way to stay sharp, something The Orium Circle need to consider. It's all well and good not wanting any sort of intense competition, but if we're not careful we'll have lost our edge if and when another enemy raises its head."

"Good point," Jalem acknowledges, "but there are much easier ways of staying sharp, Conrad, like what Jacob's doing with his class. Rucklz on a grand scale ... all the competition you need."

"It's just a thought," Noah concludes, wanting to climb on top of the bar and let loose. "For all we know, Odin and Neve were just being their weird selves, doing the whole silent treatment thing."

"They were there for a reason," I declare, urging Noah onto the bar as Zoe Tallis makes an appearance, turning a lot of heads, "but that's for another day. Let's see if Noah can finally hit those notes."

"Here we go," Conrad mutters, grimacing in expectation of another racket.

As Noah gets the crowd's attention, he clears his throat, throwing a glance in Zoe Tallis' direction. She's kind enough to smile at his mild obsession, showing no signs of genuine interest. Not that this put's Noah off as he belts out the first lines of a famous Society tune.

He signals for the merry members to sing along which they dutifully do, laughing and clinking glasses as Noah hits full stride, failing to hit a single note. The cheers explode in Rebel's Rest as the song ends, Noah jumping down from the bar to a round of applause.

"Well ...?" he asks as he always does, leaving Harvey to choose his words carefully.

"Just checking, were you singing *Give me Remedy ...?*"

I burst out laughing with the others as Noah gets Harvey in a headlock, rubbing the top of his head until he's rubbing thin air .... Harvey using the Disira charm to escape ... re-appearing for a proposed duet.

"Well, *come on*, then," Harvey calls over to us, understanding there's no duel without the agreed duet.

Conrad offers me a nervous grin, stepping onto the bar with visions of flight and fury urging him on. We shuffle closer together, taken along by the slow clapping and raised glasses, the song we all know ringing around us: *The Ballad of Rebel's Rest.*

It's a ridiculous song about the wizards who refused to leave the place we're in now, singing until the Society elders gave in. We sing along with the crowd, adding ridiculous gestures to raise the spirits: a group of friends who meet up to do normal teenage things, like staying out late and planning things to give adults sleepless nights.

THE GROUND FLOOR OF THE CENDRYLL RESTS IN DARKNESS, the Quij asleep on the bookshelves underneath the skylight — their beautiful glow not needed in the witching hours. It's close to 3 a.m. Rebel's Rest finally kicking us out when the owner couldn't keep his eyes open. More like *kicked through* to be precise, the string on the lamps lining the walls used to transport us home.

Home is The Cendryll — the place I've never really left and have no intention of leaving. Jacob's got my mum's room on the fifth floor, and I stay in the room vacated by Kaira's aunt, Philomeena. A teenage girl needs her space, after all, but this doesn't extend to night time visits from a certain boy, pinching my waist to get the desired reaction.

We've got The Cendryll to ourselves at this hour. It's

been a long day and there are things to discuss, not least Conrad's growing interest in a duel that could get us into hot water. The least we'll have to do is discuss it with Casper and Philomeena.

As we head to The Seating Station, I take Conrad's hand and lead him to Quandary Corner — an isolated seating area that rests in the shadows. Some places resonate, almost taking you back to the time you wish you had again. Quandary Corner was *my* place; *our* place where the endless wonders began.

I steal a quick kiss once we're perched in Quandary Corner, feeling more comfortable that it's out of view of the spiral staircase. The Seating Station provides more space but not the secrecy required, so we cuddle up in Quandary Corner, looking up at the skylight filled with stars, happy to sit together while the rest of the faculty sleeps.

Churchill is still here: Kaira's cat. He always senses our presence so will appear at the top of the spiral staircase soon. Until then, my focus is on a boy with a renewed purpose: to prove his gift for flight once more.

"It could be dangerous," I say as Conrad pulls me closer.

"Only up to a point. We're allies after all, making it a perfect platform for sky rider training. I mean, look at what we learnt in Gilweean, free falling from our Williynx and spiralling through tunnels of ice toward the earth. If this plays out, we might have found another training ground."

"I say we track them first ... see how The Domitus tame the Riadek, then we decide on the duel. It's got to fit within Society parameters, you know that, and that means no inciting of conflict. We're not immune from banishment."

"Fair enough," he says, looking up at the skylight.

"You think you can take them, don't you?" I prompt,

studying his intense expression. "Beat them in a friendly battle."

Conrad nods. "I can hold my own in the skies, but it's more about missing the intensity of battle: the adrenaline rush."

"Let's just make sure Odin and Neve aren't drawing us into a trap first."

"Like what?"

"Like an 'accident' in the skies, spreading the fear that forced Alice Aradel out of hiding."

~

THE EXPECTED CONVERSATIONS BEGIN EARLY NEXT MORNING AS The Cendryll bursts into life, the Quij floating down to offer their morning greeting.

We'd stayed up all night, only catching sleep in the few hours before dawn. Sometimes, it's nice to just be away from things, tucked up in a familiar location. That's what I wanted last night after our return from Rebel's Rest: to capture the magic of a spectacular universe at rest.

We get to our feet as the doors start to swing open, welcoming familiar faces to the bustling faculty responsible for remedies. The traffic is as busy leaving through the doors, either returning to above-ground duties in the many shops or simply wanting a dose of normality.

It's not something I miss, the everyday existence of a world devoid of magic. I thought I'd miss my friends when I found out about the S.P.M.A. but they were few and far between in the first place — the ones I did see above ground struggling to find things to talk about.

Most friendships are fickle, anyway, based on circumstances and convenience. I know how lucky I've been with the friends I've got now, beginning with Kaira's appearance: a friend I hope I'll see soon. For now, it's time to discuss the rumours of a duel with Kaira's dad and aunt — Casper and Philomeena — who move in their graceful manner near the spiral staircase.

They spend time with talkative Cendryll members they once kept their distance from. A lot has changed since then, including the sky urchins offering advice to the youngest amongst us: Jacob's class of inquisitive students who're desperate to pass their trial, determining whether they stay or leave.

Yoran has endless patience, an elderly sky urchin currently explaining the powers and limitations of a Disira charm to Ethan Lyell. Ethan is clever but relies on his charm and good looks. It's dawning on him that he's in a fierce competition with his classmates — none of them keen to give the other an advantaged. They've got a lot to learn about the power of unity.

As Ethan reaches out for a book delivered by a bottle-blue Quij, he keeps time with Yoran, running over the key principles of the Disira charm. He's got all the hallmarks of a Renn except for the intensity which, I imagine, will come in time. His great uncle and aunt, Casper and Philomeena, stop to talk to him, asking how he's settling in. He *loves* it here but is also under no illusions. Family names give you no advantage: you cut it or you don't.

Ageing giants and Williynx are the other two new additions to The Cendryll, a flurry of feathers filling the hollow chamber each morning. Kerevenn is the most regular face on the ground floor, his thin, stooped figure now dressed in light blue, discarding the grey uniform of Sad Souls: the land of ageing giants.

Hovering near The Seating Station, Kerevenn is still

negotiating his way into the hearts of the Society elders, working out the subtle rhythms of The Cendryll as he offers assistance to whoever needs it. He hasn't worked out that he doesn't work for anyone here; he's an equal, still struggling to come to terms with this after decades at the beck-and-call of senior Society members.

Kerevenn looked after my mum after her 'mishap': the reason she's not allowed here anymore. His kindness is part of his interaction with others, and it was this very kindness that stopped my mum falling into the hands of those wanting revenge. Mum had a power complex, treating others like underlings and being unnecessarily cruel. Not many people ask about her now: a sign of the hurt she caused.

The other reason she's still got some form of protection, hidden in the twisted building on the Society margins, is down to Casper and Philomeena Renn. Unlike my mum, they've always worn their power with ease: a mark of those with a calling.

"Glad to see you made it home," Philomeena says with a smile, her maternal instincts keeping an eye on me.

"It's Conrad's fault; he started singing."

Casper raises his eyebrows. "*Singing*?"

"To win a bet," Conrad explains, rubbing his eyes in an attempt to stay alert.

"So we hear," Casper adds, the handsome, mixed-race features offering a look of caution. "A duel is highly unlikely to get the approval of The Orium Circle, Conrad. After all, you're talking about competing with creatures only recently tamed."

"It would be a way to stay sharp, though."

"Maybe," Philomeena adds, "but it sends the wrong

message: that conflict is still a common feature of Society interaction."

"We were thinking of visiting Drandok," I say as I stand, keen to get in the shower. "To see how they tame the Riadek."

"No harm in that," Casper adds, studying us as he takes out a Follygrin: a sign he knows we're up to something.

13

A QUESTION OF INTENT

Talk of Drandok gains pace later in the day after we offer greetings to other familiar faces. Noah and Lucy arrive in The Cendryll through one of the many doors lining the ground floor, having received word of our meeting via Scribberals.

Noah and Lucy are based in a different Society faculty — The Leverin — so Scribberals are used to communicate meeting points before another evening of Night Ranging begins.

Jacob's also present, having taken the rest of the day off. He wants his students to experience various teaching methods: Farraday on hand to remind the class of the beauty and danger of all magical things.

According to Jacob, the students fell into complete silence when Farraday entered the small classroom on the second floor for the first time, their awe-struck gazes falling onto a wizard who's scarred body tells its own tale.

Part of me suspects that Jacob's taken the morning off after hearing rumours of our planned duel in Drandok. Ever the protective older brother, he still appears when he's worried about me, offering gentle reassurance and guidance whenever he feels the need.

The question of darker rhythms leads the conversation, the five of us gathered around the dining table in the middle of the room. I love the elegance and eccentricity of my personal space in The Cendryll, inherited from Philomeena who spends less time here now. Velvet sofas sit in each corner of the room and a collection of Quij flutter in the kitchen, illuminating a space that seems to stretch to the heavens.

Lunch has been made by Conrad, the steak and salad gobbled down, everyone present keen to discuss our meeting with Odin and Neve last night. There's being detached and being altogether shifty, not that shady people don't exist in the Society: they do.

Once doubt is cast, all Society eyes turn their attention to potential misdeeds, committed to maintaining peace where magic, adventure and wonder can flourish. Adventure is the topic of conversation at the dining table perched in the centre of the room. Conrad's steak and salad has gone down a treat and with Jacob washing up, we get to the topic of duels.

"So, Casper didn't look too happy about the idea of a duel?" Noah comments, turning to look for seconds in the kitchen. Unfortunately, he's out of luck.

"Taking out his Follygrin wasn't a coincidence," I reply. "He wanted to make a point that we're still being watched."

"We're watched more than you realise," Jacob states from the kitchen, blowing bubbles to the Quij who hover high above. "Not out of suspicion but protection. Let's not forget, we're still some of the youngest members in the Society, and being Night Rangers doesn't put you above the law."

"*Obviously*," I reply with a touch of annoyance. "It's just a *duel*, Jacob ... similar to the one you had earlier on The Hallowed Lawn. *That* got a little violent, didn't it, so don't get all high-and-mighty on us."

Jacob returns to the table, handing Noah a glass of white liquid: Semphul to abate hunger for a boy with hollow legs. "Agreed, Guppy. It did get a little out of hand on The Hallowed Lawn this morning, making me more grateful you and Conrad agreed to help.

The difference is, *Rucklz* is a *game*; taming Riadek *isn't* and nor is tempting The Domitus into a duel. They're humourless soldiers who only have one mode of training: ferocity. Things could turn ugly very quickly."

"You seem to be forgetting that Conrad's the best sky rider in the Society," I add, feeling a little defensive. Conrad *is* pushing the boundaries with his idea for a duel, but we've experienced far more dangerous things.

Taming Riadek will be *brilliant* to see, and then there's Drandok itself: a realm Society folk don't clamour to visit. I suppose the idea of ferocious creatures, roaring as they fight against their instructors, doesn't fill people with joy. I've always been drawn to danger, though, meaning I'm probably not destined for a long life.

"Easy, Guppy," Conrad says, swiping the glass from Noah's hand and finishing off the Semphul remedy. "Jacob's just being protective and he's got a point; the last thing we want to do is stir up trouble."

"*Exactly*," Noah echoes, patting his stomach in the hope there's more of the hunger remedy on offer. "What's the point of picking a fight with the Domitus? Let's just keep things as they are: a lot of fun and a little bit of work."

"So, we ignore how weird they were in The Shallows?" Lucy counters.

"Why not? *Lots* of people are weird, Lucy, including you."

Lucy offers Noah a sarcastic smile, finishing off her steak as slowly as possible as Noah eyes it longingly.

"I say we travel to Drandok to check things out," Conrad adds, standing as he does so. "It'll be cool to watch them tame Riadek: a mystery in itself."

"So, you're not looking for an argument?" Jacob asks, sitting at the end of the dining table — always the paternal voice of concern.

"No one's looking for an argument, Jacob," I reply, "but if their visit to The Shallows was what I think it was, we'll be up to any challenge they've got in mind."

"What, like a duel?"

"If they want to play with fire," I reply, which seems to put an end to the debate, leaving Jacob to say his goodbyes, returning to the second floor to see how his students are fairing under Farraday's tutelage.

"He looks a bit miffed," Noah states as Jacob closes the door behind him.

"I think he misses the madness," I reply with a smile, looking forward to a trip to a land where monsters are tamed.

~

DRANDOK RESTS BETWEEN THE ROYISIN HEIGHTS AND Saraseai Lake. Its inhabitants take on a number of roles, some taming Riadek while others roam beyond The Society Sphere, using their intimidating presence to ensure mischief doesn't morph into malice. That's the official line, anyway.

Night Rangers and sleeping soldiers commit to part-time

duties, wanting the freedom to enjoy everything the S.P.M.A. has to offer. That's where I fit in: a witch with a thirst for life, my attention divided between Society duties and romantic ones. On that note, I keep a close eye on Conrad who seems increasingly agitated.

Olin and Neve Blin have got under his skin — an unspoken challenge he won't be able to ignore. A duel in the sky, even with tamed Silverbacks, is a dangerous one and if things get out of hand, there'll be consequences. Being part of the Society army doesn't get you any special treatment, mainly because most members fight in one way or another.

Some of us meet conflict head on whereas others operate behind the scenes — in faculties where new charms, artefacts and remedies are created: magic for all eventualities. With a challenge on the horizon, I study the fading light outside the dining room window. Soon, it will be time to take to the air once again, to a place where ferocious creatures are tamed.

As day fades into early evening, I take a surveillance device out of my trouser pocket. A Panorilum looks like a normal book until you throw it into the air. Once in the air, it unfolds into a large sheet of parchment paper. The parchment hangs in mid-air formed of multiple sections the size of the original book. Each section can show whatever you want to see: people's whereabouts, possible issues within the Society and all magical realms.

Drandok is the realm in question so Noah, Lucy, Conrad and I sit at the dining table, studying the illustration that fills the Panorilum ... drawn to the mountains framing a space most accurately described as a chamber for captured creatures ... Riadek struggling in chains as the Domitus assert their control of them.

It looks pretty brutal, to be honest, the Silverbacks

roaring as they whip their wings against the chains ... some breaking out and escaping to the skies ... only to have their flight limited by the group of Society soldiers who stand in a circle below... emotionless as they struggle to contain a ferocious creature's fury. I'm not sure who's idea it was to tame dangerous creatures, but it doesn't look like it's going entirely to plan.

"No wonder they never smile," Noah comments as we study the figures darting for cover as a Silverback trashes out its wings in fury. "Imagine *that* as a job."

"It makes you wonder who'd sign up to be a Domitus," Lucy adds, her slender frame hiding an iron will.

"Witches and wizards with a point to prove," Conrad says, getting up from his chair to stand right next to the Panorilum. He kneels to study the taming range surrounded by mountains. "Maybe they lost their nerve in the last war, choosing to hide in places like Gilweean instead of stepping into battle."

"Or maybe they just like violence," I counter, "and Drandok is the perfect place for them."

Conrad pauses and turns to me, seeming distant. "It could be another way the Society's managing potential dangers, Guppy, allowing volatile witches and wizards to let off steam."

"Makes sense," Noah adds, joining Conrad alongside the Panorilum. "Give them an outlet to stop their violent tendencies spilling inwards."

"Avoiding another Erent Koll," Lucy echoes — everyone present knowing full well how *that* ended.

"So, when are we going?" I ask, getting a little restless cooped up in The Cendryll. As great as the faculty for remedies is, it's basically home and who wants to sit at *home all day*, staring at places you'd rather visit.

Drandok isn't likely to be a barrel of laughs, but it will tell us more about the nature of the Domitus. Why they choose such a dangerous job, for example, and what makes them so humourless.

"Let's make it the first place to visit tonight," Lucy replies, determined to put this 'duel' thing to bed.

Duel or no duel, we'll arrive in Drandok on our trusted Williynx: Night Rangers on a mission to learn the art of taming monsters, while keeping an eye out for the humourless pair who appeared in Poridian Parlour last night.

14

DRANDOK

Evening falls and we gather on the ground floor of The Cendryll, happy to be alone before our journey to Drandok begins. Conversation regarding the potential dangers of a duel faded after it became clear it was intensifying Conrad's desire.

All Night Rangers are competitive, to a degree, but Conrad takes things to another level. Part of me thinks it's linked to losing his dad in the last war and the *way* Theodore died ... sacrificing his life in the final phase to secure the Society's future.

If I'm being honest, I think Conrad bears a secret grudge towards the surviving malevs who vanished when the smoke of war settled, hoping to find a safe haven beyond The Society Sphere. The vastness of the realms existing beyond the S.P.M.A. makes it relatively easy to hide out for a while, but eventually we track them down, leaving it up to The Orium Circle to decide what the punishment should be.

Sometimes, karma takes care of things, like it did with The Sinister Four: the first bullies I met. They used to run the Society library — known as The Pancithon — flexing their Society clout at every opportunity. Their humiliation of Jacob in our early days here stuck with me, so when they all perished in the last brutal battle, I didn't shed a tear. Things are very different now, obviously, so we have to tread carefully on our journey to Drandok.

We've covered our bases by mentioning it to Casper and Philomeena Renn — the two figures you *definitely don't* want to cross in The Cendryll. We might be Night Rangers but they're *legends*, and when it comes to a matter of judgement The Orium Circle will almost always side with members who have seen and sacrificed so much.

Casper and Philomeena fit into this category so with the clear sense our journey will be watched by them, we ready ourselves for a meeting with the emotionless group who frequent Drandok.

"Ready?" Lucy asks as we take our positions on the edge of the S.P.M.A. logo, dominating the ground floor of The Cendryll.

With a nod from us all, we raise our arms towards the skylight situated directly above, releasing the Spintz charm. Light streaks of colourful energy float towards the skylight ... blue, amber, purple and yellow ... until they touch the surface, covering the skylight with a kaleidoscope of colour.

It's our calling card to the Williynx: our feathered companions who never fail to arrive when duty calls. They neither belong to us nor have to respond to our calls, but as long as our intentions are in the interests of the Society, they always have and always will.

I offer Conrad a smile as our arms remained raised, hoping to see his expression soften: a signal he *isn't* looking for trouble in Drandok. There's something I can't quite put my finger on about his demeanour ... as if he's struggling with an immovable thought ... that the two figures who engaged in a stare down in Poridian Parlour are connected to us in some way, but *how*?

The light begins to shimmer above, signalling the impending arrival of our Williynx, and moments later they appear through the skylight ... the glass turning into liquid form at the touch of their feathers. Our feathered friends glide down in an elegant quartet: fire-red, yellow, turquoise and powder blue. It's time for the evening surveillance to begin.

We climb onto our Williynx, tapping our legs lightly against their bodies to signal flight and off we go, rising through the hollow chamber of The Cendryll towards the skylight we vanish through seconds later.

THE EVENING SKIES ARE RELATIVELY QUIET, SILHOUETTES OF other Night Rangers in the distance, moving towards the realms within their remit — realms beyond the eyes of the above-ground world which operates on its own axis of unimaginative routine. We fly in a synchronised line, passing over Society Square before we reach its margins.

The people entering and leaving buildings are mainly Society members locking up for the evening, either returning to their above-ground dwellings or disappearing into the recesses of the shops ... through Periums and the faculties they're attached to.

I press my face against Laieya's blue feathers as the wind lifts, listening to her heartbeat as we pick up speed. We blaze past The Winter Quarter and beyond, seeking out a realm few of us have spent any time in: Noah being the exception. It's the reason Noah recognised Olin and Neve

Blin when they appeared in Poridian Parlour, looking out of place the moment they sat at the table in the corner.

Noah's brief visit to Drandok was to check on the condition of the soldiers said to be hiding the extent of their injuries — injuries sustained in battle or their taming of the Riadek. As always, the Domitus offered little, taking Noah and his old Night Ranger crowd to the stone shelters the soldiers were recuperating in.

Healing remedies such as Srynx Serum were soaking into their skin, bandages covering arms and legs to either accelerate the healing or cover up deeper wounds. Tonight will tell us more now the Domitus have decided to leave their realm, stepping into less depressing places like The Shallows, looking for company or trouble.

With my hair lifting as we fly through the dark skies, I look along the line formed by my Night Ranger comrades ... a touch of excitement rising in me at the thought of meeting Olin and Neve Blin again. Bullies don't last long in the Society so if they end up falling into this category, they'll be dealt with accordingly.

"Quivvens at the ready," Conrad says, sensing we're closing in on Drandok.

A Quivven is what we use for protection once we're beyond The Society Sphere, the colour of our penchant stones fading as we do so. A Quivven is a small, brass hexagon that you push into your flesh — not as bad as it sounds.

Once buried safely, it glows in the colour of your penchant stone, mine glowing a bright blue underneath my right wrist. I doubt we're going to need any protection, but no Society soldier ignores their instincts. Drandok deals in danger — of the creature kind — so it's better to be safe than sorry.

THE MOUNTAINS FRAMING DRANDOK DOMINATE THE NIGHT sky. I can just make out cells cut into the stone at the foot of the mountains where, I imagine, the Riadek are kept. We choose to stay in the sky on our arrival, lighting up the darkness with a string of Promesiun charms: ribbons of light to signal solidarity. Whatever awaits us below, our focus is investigation.

If we end up in a fire fight, it will be in retaliation to an attack. A duel is to be avoided, if possible, our aim to see exactly how the ferocious Silverbacks are tamed and the cost of such a choice. Authorised by the S.P.M.A., it's a job that attracts a certain type of character.

Strings of light appear from the ground, circling as they rise above the mountains, followed by an incredible roar flooding the air as one of the cells cut into the mountains opens — the sight of a vast, armoured creature whipping against its chains ready to face its captors once more.

"Slow and steady," I say, nodding for us to make our descent, our Quivvens glowing underneath our skin as we do.

"Still in the mood for a duel?" Noah prompts, glancing at Conrad who remains silent on the back of his turquoise Williynx, clearly troubled by a recurring thought he can't shake.

Our descent continues, staying within the rings of light that hover above the mountains: a taming chamber acting as safe space for submission. There's no sign of Odin and Neve Blin yet so I study the figures in grey, circling the restricted Silverback. As black smoke appears from their hands, I begin to understand how they work their magic ... a combination of pure and dark charms ... authorised by The Orium Circle to contain threats.

This in itself isn't a shock. One of the key changes to Society law was the acceptance that dark magic could not simply be banned and ignored: it had to be mastered and understood, to be used in exceptional circumstances.

How and *when* it should be applied is a more complex question, the distorted power of Gorrah (dark magic) having a hypnotising effect on underworld creatures. Something about the sight of black smoke — a symbol of the Niavak curse — makes me uneasy, though.

It's cruel and unnecessary ... as if the Domitus are enjoying punishing the Silverback which roars in pain. There are other ways to tame giants so I kick my legs against Laieya, instructing my Williynx to descend further, ready to engage the emotionless soldiers in more than distant recognition.

"*Guppy?*" comes Conrad's call, but I don't look back, my instinctive dislike of cruelty kicking in. Maybe a duel is going to be needed after all.

As I hover above the taming cell, I feel the tension in Laieya's body, her powder-blue feathers standing to attention at the sight of a threat below. My whispered reassurances are enough to keep her in position, holding off any sudden ice blasts that will trigger carnage.

With Conrad, Lucy and Noah appearing alongside me, I signal towards the black smoke filling the cell ... the sight of the Domitus' faces covered by a web, courtesy of the Weveris charm.

"They're *enjoying it*," I say as another roar rips through the sky. "Who needs to use a Niavak curse to tame an injured Silverback already in chains?"

"You don't know that, Guppy," Lucy says, her expression suggesting concern.

I can tell she thinks I'm going to do something stupid, but she's wrong. My days of impulsive reaction are behind me — experience teaching me that it often leads to more problems than it solves. We're here to study the art of taming: a dark art, in my opinion, making me wonder how much the Society elders know about the precise methods of taming used, and if they even care.

Some could argue that you have to fight fire with fire, meaning the use of curses to mute a dangerous creature's venom is acceptable, but where does *that* trend lead...? I know *exactly* where: down paths we don't need to go again.

"Take it easy, Guppy," Conrad states as he moves alongside me on his turquoise Williynx. "Let's find a place to rest in the mountains, making it clear we're not leaving anytime soon. Then we descend when the performance is over, giving us a chance to work out what's *really* going on."

"It's not as if The Orium Circle doesn't know what's going on here," Noah adds as we manoeuvre our feathered companions to the mountain face, looking for a platform to witness a strange sorcery from.

"You'd think," Lucy replies.

"Unless they're authorising torture, that is," I counter, "which is what this is."

"Let's just wait this out to find out more," Conrad suggests, climbing off his Williynx once we reach a platform to rest on. "Look, the smoke's dying away now they realise we're watching them. I guarantee Olin and Neve are down there somewhere, hiding in whatever secret spaces the mountains offer."

"What are you thinking, Conrad?" Noah prompts.

"That they planned this whole thing to get us out here."

"What for?"

Conrad doesn't reply but no reply is needed, and as I sit alongside him I ready myself for the conflict awaiting us below.

"It's a *performance*," I say to break the silence, our Quivvens glowing in the darkness. "A performance to make us react, drawing us into a situation that can be turned against us."

"Looks like someone down there's got a grudge," Lucy adds.

"*Exactly*," Conrad replies, swinging his legs over the mountain edge, "so let's give them something to think about."

With that, he stands and whispers 'Weveris', releasing a vast, black web that he directs towards the Silverback who staggers under the cursed smoke, shrieking in pain. He's skilled enough to camouflage the web, masking it in the evening light until it falls over the Silverback.

As the injured creature's roars intensify, Conrad turns to us, already in position astride our Williynx, nodding for the final descent to begin, towards our meeting with a strange breed of soldier drawn to cruelty and domination.

15

TAMING FURY

The figure who meets us on the ground is less than welcoming, maintaining a degree of civility expected of all Society members. Dressed in grey trousers and a loose-fitting shirt worn by all Domitus, the bearded figure waits for us to dismount from our Williynx before speaking.

"You have no authority to interfere with our procedures."

I study the small group with him, recognising none of them. There are more Domitus guarding the cages built into the mountain walls — the imprisoned Silverbacks eyeing their captors with restrained fury. The whole place has a strange energy as if containing such a creature goes against logic, but logic changes with circumstances and The Society knows only too well the danger of ignoring dark forces.

"We have the authority to go wherever we please," Conrad replies, his tanzanite Quivven glowing in his neck.

"Which *doesn't* include interference," the bearded figure repeats, not particularly tall but striking in build, muscles bursting through his loose, grey shirt.

I doubt they'll do him much good in a firefight with witches and wizards of equal skill, but we're trying to *avoid* that so I step in, offering the bearded stranger a forced smile.

"We met two of your crew last night in The Shallows: Poridian Parlour to be exact."

"And?"

"And we thought they were up to something ... being all weird ... sitting in silence and staring us out."

"Silence is valued here, Miss Grayling."

Here goes the *Miss* again: a reminder of the contempt some Society elders have for us.

"As well as torture?" I reply, offering the bearded muscle man another smile.

His expression doesn't change. Instead, he turns to whisper to the two men on either side of him. I glance at Noah and Lucy who seem agitated by something, gesturing for me to look back. The clatter of the cage behind me suggests we've interrupted the taming process ... one that isn't going to be put on hold due to our arrival.

It's another sign of intimidation from the Domitus. With our Williynx hovering in mid-air — secret weapons should we need them — I respond as I always do in such circumstances, rising to the challenge.

"Let's see it then," I demand, holding the muscle-man's gaze.

This gets a loud laugh from the crew until I whip out a Promesiun charm to release the Riadek: my first impulsive move for a while. Sometimes, actions speak louder than words, and this action wipes the smile off their faces pretty quickly.

Noah and Lucy aren't smiling either, but I catch Conrad's expression in my peripheral vision: the boy who's aligned to me in principle and spirit. The Spintz charms remain active above us, following our movements as another roar rings through the mountains.

"*Hold*!" the bearded figure shouts to his crew, including the Domitus guarding the open cell, and they do just that, using their penchants to light up the mountain walls, preparing a retreat if necessary.

They probably don't know I've faced Riadek before — *loads* of them in The Caves of Varakel when we wiped out an even bigger monster: the Dexametris. If the Domitus think one Silverback's going to send us running, they're in for a surprise.

A flicker of light from my Promesiun charm snaps Noah and Lucy into action. "Circle the Riadek as it closes in," I instruct at the sound of the first roar. "Fire and Light to disorient it, then water to flood it back into its cell."

A nod from the others signals a familiar drill, ending with the use of the flight charm to avoid being caught in a flood of our own making. We still have the advantage of being kids in the eyes of most adults, despite our experience in battle. The half-surprised, half-contemptuous looks on the bearded soldiers' faces suggest they doubt our military skill. Well, there's no time like the present to remind more seasoned wizards of our abilities.

If they haven't worked out why I'm called The Fire Witch, they're about to find out as I whip my Promesiun charm into the air, sending it spinning close to the group of Domitus who look as though they're going to retaliate until they feel an imposing presence above them ... reminded of the power of the Williynx who can shatter bodies with blasts of ice.

The smug grins are wiped off their faces as I lift my

Promesiun charm higher into the air, whipping it in a circular motion around the group of Domitus who are forced to remain static, suffering a mild humiliation at the hands of a girl they were laughing at only minutes ago.

Their smiles have turned to expressions of mild puzzlement, wondering why my back is turned to a colossal creature pounding its hind legs on the earth as it strains against the chains containing its famed ferocity.

I know exactly where the Silverback is, keeping Conrad in my peripheral vision as I make a point to the arrogant men who inch back towards the mountain face, jumping at the sound of a roar from another cell buried in the mountain walls.

They know the consequences of retaliation ... as do the other Domitus who appear from illuminated arches in the mountain walls ... including Odin and Neve Blin who offer us the same blank stare we got at Poridian Parlour.

With everyone in play, I return to the formation of four, standing in between Conrad and Lucy with Noah opposite: a synchronised group of Night Rangers familiar with each other's rhythms, ready to put on a show for the band of soldiers conditioned in cruelty.

"Let's break the chains and give them something to think about," Conrad suggests, eyeing the muscle-bound group who watch from a distance.

I nod with a smile, confident of my magical powers and completely trusting the boy I love. We're a formidable force, and it's time to show the emotionless soldiers the consequences of courting danger. As the Riadek roars its fury, straining against the chains containing its powers, the four of us send our Promesiun charms along the ground.

We lift them inches from the Silverback's constrained,

armoured body ... the lines of light resting on the chains, infusing them with steel until the links weaken and shatter one-by-one ... allowing the Silverback to roar into life.

"*Now!*" I shout to the others who know what to do, activating the Disira charm to vanish from view, reappearing behind the freed Silverback who roars once more, sniffing for our scent along the ground as its vast, armoured wings spike with sinister intent.

Another strike with the Promesiun charm rips through the soil around the roaring Riadek, causing it to lose its footing as it tries to turn, angling to whip its armoured wings towards us, but we vanish before it can, sending a blast of fire towards it with the use of the Smekelin charm — fire that hangs like a curtain around the disoriented Silverback which shrieks at the sight of the curtain of flames engulfing it.

Unlike the crowd of Domitus who look on in silence, there is no intention to use cruelty to force a submission. In fact, our intention is the exact opposite, aiming to prove that power can be asserted in subtle ways — through common charms rather than unnecessary curses. It's just a matter of wrong footing a once-feared creature until it senses defeat, symbolised by our collective shout of 'LEVENAN' as we release a flood of water from our hands.

The water fills the taming range quickly, rising to our ankles as the curtain of fire limits the Silverback's vision. Each time it moves, the curtain closes in, the flames intensifying as it does so. It only needs the water to rise now for the point to be made: that the taming methods used are questionable, meaning the Domitus are now in our sights.

With the water rising in the taming cell, we enact the final charm, uttering 'Propellus Celiri' to rise from the ground, our legs free of the water as a flower wraps around our wrists, propelling us towards our Williynx.

Once astride our feathered companions, we tap our legs to ignite a flume of fine ice, ensuring we remain positioned over the group of stunned Domitus who can only look on, fuming at the sense they've been forced into a humiliating position of submission. The soldiers of Drandok are no match for the Williynx, remaining motionless as the water rises to their waists.

Their arms remain by their sides, their neutral position signalling no threat as we tap our legs against the Williynx once more, triggering mild blasts of ice that freeze the water surrounding the Silverback: a vision of youth and colour in the sky, causing a monster to retreat to its stone cell.

~

A COLLECTION OF COLOURFUL FEATHERS DRAINS THE WATER from the taming range, generating a line of light on the outer boundary, creating a drainage system in the soil. With our skill in the face of ferocity proven, we signal for our feathered friends to morph into smaller forms, allowing them to stay close by, hovering near our shoulders as the real conversation begins.

It's time to find out what the Domitus are *really* up to. First, two of them appear in The Shallows, entering into a staring contest with four young wizards minding their own business; then there's the use of curses to tame Silverbacks. In Conrad's words, if they want a duel, they can have one — not that it's going to distract us from finding out if more surveillance is needed in Drandok.

The Domitus seem unintelligent and predictable, down

to their mannerisms, dress code and crude forms of intimidation, and if they thought drawing us here was going to make us weaken at the knees, they've misjudged us. Whoever the leader is, he's going to need more than muscles to explain his way out of a taming ritual that uses curses.

A group of kids has just proven they're unnecessary, so unless he wants a flood of a different kind, in the form of a colossal army of Society soldiers descending on Drandok, he better start talking.

"Impressive, Miss Grayling," he offers with a sneer which soon falters when I put him straight.

"It's Guppy and I'm no *Miss*."

"Of course. And you must be Conrad: the boy gifted with flight."

"And who are you?" Conrad asks, touching the Quivven that continues to glow in his neck.

"Orgev."

"Well, Orgev, do you mind explaining why you're using curses to tame Silverbacks?"

"It's the most effective way for lasting results."

"*Lasting* meaning what?" Lucy asks, stepping forward to make sure she's noticed.

Her slight demeanour makes people misjudge her, although I think Orgev's getting the point; we're not leaving until we get answers.

"Taming is a process of steps ... the Niavak curse used *mildly* in the final phase."

"Why...?" Noah challenges, pulling the top off a vial of orange liquid: Srynx Serum for mild wounds, applied to the small burns he's acquired from using the fire charm.

"Because the Riadek needs to be *diminished* for its powers to be permanently altered. Everything we do is authorised by the Society. The Orium Circle visit regularly to carry out checks."

"And do The Orium Circle know some of your soldiers are riding around The Society Sphere on Silverbacks…?" I ask. "Like those two who are hiding back there."

"There's no law against this," Orgev replies, the smug smile returning.

"And is there a law against duels?" Conrad prompts, "because something tells me your comrades tracked us to The Shallows, looking for something."

"And what would that be?"

"A challenge," Conrad replies with increased intent. "I mean, it must get boring out here, firing curses at creatures in chains. Not much of a challenge, is it?"

Orgev's smug smile fades, replaced with the emotionless glare we were faced with in Poridian Parlour. "We should remember we are on the same side, Conrad, sacrificing many things for peace."

Conrad takes a step closer, studying the muscle-men surrounding Orgev. "That's funny," he begins, "because I get the feeling you're up to something out here, making me wonder if you're the people Alice Aradel is hiding from. After all, the evening witch has lost her powers, relying on desperate trades to keep her going. All of a sudden, she risks capture to get her hands on a few Zombuls…?"

"False accusation is a serious offence, Conrad."

"And so is abuse of power, Orgev, so you'll let us look around or we'll come back with an army."

"And you think you have that power?"

I step alongside Conrad, holding Orgev's smug gaze before adding, "Well, we know a man who does … Casper Renn … who's watching all of this in The Cendryll."

That changes things, Orgev faltering at the sound of

Casper Renn's name: a man who's fought and defeated every threat in recent history. I'm sure he's studying us now, watching as we stare down the group who realise they've got a decision to make: truth or dare.

16

CURSED FLIGHT

The mild tension in the air eases as Orgev offers us another smile, this one a little more genuine.

"So, what would you like to see?" he asks, gesturing around him to the mountain walls framing the taming range. "We can take you closer to the cells, offering you reassurance that cruelty is not the aim of our taming procedures. We can also give you a more general tour within the mountains, where we live when based here. Otherwise, we can show you Drandok from the skies."

Conrad doesn't bite at the obvious bait — his desire to test himself against the Domitus currently under control.

"Maybe, the grand tour later," I say, replying before male ego gets out of hand. "What about showing us inside to give us a sense of the place? Then we could watch a taming procedure from start to finish, giving us the reassurances we need."

"As you wish, Guppy," Orgev replies, buttoning the top of his loose grey shirt in a gesture of odd formality. He's either patronising us with his sudden desire to please or there's more to it: a leader possibly worrying about what could be revealed.

I haven't got Conrad's sense about the place yet, whistling for Laieya to hover close by as we head towards the mountain crevice in the east wall. Unlike the Silverbacks caged in their stone cells, our Williynx can shape shift into any form, making them an unpredictable threat to those on the wrong end of their fury.

The Domitus know the Williynx well, the frequent glances from Orgev and his crew a sign of their wariness. After all, one blast of ice from a Williynx can shatter a body beyond recognition. We're not here to start an argument — as much as Conrad would like to — but to get clarity on the intent of two figures who appeared in Poridian Parlour.

Whatever the reason, we're about to find out more as we follow Orgev's crew through the mountain crevice, leading us into a labyrinth of spaces housing a strange silence. The spaces appear at the end of a winding walkway, the mountain crevice expanding the further we walk, leading to open rooms decorated in various ways.

Male and female figures occupy the rooms ... rooms which remind me of the cells the Silverbacks are trapped in at the foot of the mountains. Drandok isn't a prison but it isn't a holiday camp either, making me wonder who would choose such an existence.

A female figure steps behind a curtain hanging in her colourful space. As she does, I see the glimmer of glass on the other side ... glass that forms the wall looking out over the mountains. It's not just any window, though, it's an illustrated window — every pane presenting the viewer with a vision of a particular Society location.

The woman places her hand on the pane in the top right-hand corner, running her fingers along the outline of a realm I don't recognise. With our Williynx fluttering nearby, maintaining their minuscule forms, our tour of the silent sanctuary continues.

"What's she doing?" Noah asks, glancing at his rumbling belly.

"Looks like she's remembering something," Lucy replies, "or someone."

"*Stalking* someone, you mean," Noah adds, apologising when he accidentally steps on Orgev's foot.

The Domitus might be extending their hospitality but it's a forced gesture, not forgetting we've barged into their home, implying certain things about their rituals.

"Eiola was once a Night Ranger like yourself," Orgev explains, nodding to the comrade closest to him to add some well-needed illumination to proceedings. The comrade presses the palms of his hands against the mountain walls, causing a string of light to appear.

The light runs from his hand along the wall ... a line of light which stretches into a web of illumination, decorating the inner sanctum of Drandok with a softer tone. The soft light glowing on the walls makes me reconsider the silence here, the realisation forming that we're in the presence of trauma, not danger.

"She looks lost," Conrad whispers to me, picking up on what I sense: that Drandok is a realm where the traumatised arrive to tame their inner demons.

This leads me to a second thought ... that the taming of the Silverbacks is a test of the Domitus, assessing whether their grief has the potential to morph into venom.

"Drandok can be described as a place for the lost," states the oldest of the bearded soldiers, broad but without the excessive muscle of his comrades. He's striking to look at —

the hollow cheeks accentuating grey eyes that seem to look beyond you.

"Like Sad Souls," Lucy says, raising a hand to a young man sat cross-legged to our left.

His cell is decorated with drawings of infamous Society creatures — enemies that still haunt him, maybe.

"In some ways," replies the older figure, "although Sad Souls is for the fallen whereas Drandok caters to the brave."

"Why do they come here?" I ask, feeling guilty that I judged this silent group too soon.

"To mend significant wounds: psychological rather than physical."

"Shell shock, you mean?" Noah asks, moving a little easier through the strange hotel for troubled legends."

"Yes," Orgev replies, running his hand along a string of lights illuminating our way. "Trauma that can't easily be shaken."

"Is it why you don't smile that much?" Conrad asks as his intense gaze softens.

We've misjudged Drandok, it seems, and the people who live here. I still want to know more about Odin and Neve Blin, though, and why they sought us out in Poridian Parlour. Maybe they're as traumatised as everyone else here, sitting in the small spaces they call home, studying the illustrations on the windows that provide memories of better times. There's still the use of the curses to be explained, something that still doesn't feel right, so I ask the question.

"So, just so I understand, traumatised soldiers *choose* to come to Drandok?"

Orgev nods, offering handshakes to the inhabitants who are confident enough to step out onto the walkway. "Yes, Guppy. There is no dishonour in suffering the consequences of war, something the Society has worked very hard to ensure. In the past, soldiers were left to fight on or return to less dangerous pursuits in faculties and peaceful realms.

The issue with this, of course, was that we left damaged witches and wizards to roam with their ghosts, haunted by visions they couldn't escape. The most damaged became dangerous, eventually rising to pose our greatest threat."

"Erent Koll," I mutter, remembering the evil energy of the man we confronted in The Saralin Sands.

"Indeed, Guppy — Erent Koll and his kind. The Society has learnt many things since the last war, including distinguishing between the damaged and the damned."

"The damned?" Lucy asks, shaking the hand of the tall lady who nods as we pass, whispering indecipherable words.

"Those who become bitter," Orgev explains. "Angry at the price they've paid, marked for life in various ways. I can see you're troubled by our use of curses on the Silverbacks."

"It seems unnecessary," Conrad adds as sunlight falls onto the illustrated windows to our right, offering further illumination on our tour. "I know we jumped to conclusions; I shouldn't have assumed wrongdoing."

"It's an easy assumption to make, young Conrad," the eldest of our bearded guides replies, offering a reassuring smile. "The Society spent years tracking and punishing those engaging in dark magic; it's only natural that you'd be suspicious of our practices."

"So, why do you use curses on the Silverbacks?" Lucy asks, taking in the surroundings which suggest calm, not malice.

"To make the critical distinction," Orgev explains, "between the damaged and the damned."

M. Req"Precisely, Noah. The one thing to test a person's hidden motives is power. Gorrah — dark magic — feeds off resentment and bitterness, turning such feelings into malevolent thoughts."

"So, the curse is more for the soldiers who arrive here," I add, realising how wrong we've been about Drandok, "testing their intentions."

"Correct."

"And the ones who don't pass the test?" Conrad asks, already sensing the answer.

"Those with malice in their souls become unpredictable until they make a mistake, leading to the obvious outcome."

The Velynx, I think, imagining the fate awaiting those too damaged to heal, disturbed thoughts making them increasingly dangerous.

"Are there any Domitus you suspect of harbouring resentment towards the Society?" I ask, picking up on Orgev's changing expression.

"Two who roam without purpose," Orgev adds, pausing on our tour as we approach an enormous illustrated window, decorating the west wall of the mountain hollow. "You may have seen them in The Shallows recently."

Orgev already knows about Odin and Neve Blin, making me wonder if he's been expecting our visit.

"We saw them on our arrival here," Conrad adds, seemingly irritated whenever he thinks of them.

"Yes, Conrad. They are rarely at ease here, meaning their future path is unclear."

"What's their problem?"

Orgev looks at Conrad and me before adding, "You."

~

IT TURNS OUT ODIN AND NEVE BLIN LOST A LOT OF RELATIVES in the last war, and they blame us for their deaths. Whoever the Blin members were who lost their lives, they chose the side of darkness: malevs aligning themselves with evil. Their dead relatives did their best to *kill us*, but were ultimately unsuccessful.

Feeling more at ease in Drandok now, we stand by the large illustrated window at the west end of the illuminated space. Illustrated windows are designed to show multiple scenes, usually from different faculties or magical realms. All the scenes on this window are from the realm we're currently in: visions of taming and healing.

The image I'm looking at shows another taming range ... triangular in shape ... a Silverback crashing into the mountain face as it attempts flight. Orgev runs his hand along the steel frame of the window, causing each pane to blend into a single image of an outside space, and a familiar roar.

I recognise Odin and Neve Blin straight away, hovering in the sky on the back of their Silverbacks — as emotionless as ever. They're overseeing the release of other Silverbacks into the sky, ready to recondition the weakened beasts in the air. Conrad steps closer to me, studying every move the two Domitus make, searching for a clue to their true intentions. Are they damaged beyond repair or troubled soldiers trying to recover from battle?

Every move they make is marked with frustration, jerking their Silverbacks into position as they track the released Riadek: the official name for Silverbacks. They use a collection of charms and curses to control their flight path — two silent wizards with vengeance in their eyes.

"Still want that duel, Conrad?" Noah says, offering his best friend a half-smile.

Conrad doesn't reply, more interested in the process of taming in the skies: a sky rider who understands the human-creature bond. "They're not at one with them,"

Conrad states, placing his right hand on the window. "Everything's *forced* … as if they're taking their anger out on the Silverbacks."

"An interesting observation, Conrad," comes Orgev's reply. "You have a legendary connection to your Williynx."

"You should feel *aligned* to your creature," Conrad continues as his eyes narrow: a suspicion returning. "They're completely disconnected from their Silverbacks, and look at how they release the Niavak curse … in a wave not a whisper. It's all *too crude: too forced.*"

"Your friend mentions a duel?" came the voice of the eldest of our guides.

"Conrad thinks Odin and Neve were trying to draw us into something," Lucy explains, throwing me a concerned glance.

We both know what's coming next.

"As if they were drawing you here," Orgev adds, rubbing his beard as he studies the black smoke filling the air: cursed smoke tracking weakened, disoriented creatures through the sky.

"Exactly," Conrad replies, stepping back from the window, "and what better way than a duel to find out their true intentions?"

17

SUBTLE SORCERY

We leave the illustrated window and enter the mountain crevice to our left, leading us to another taming range where our silent foes await. Olin and Neve lead the taming in the sky: a procedure to condition weakened Silverbacks to comply to their new masters. I still don't like the methods the Domitus use, but the Riadek are fierce creatures, able to rip a human to shreds with one swipe of their wings.

At the end of the day, it's not my decision and if taming dangerous creatures is what we do now, it's not for me to argue. I'm more interested in the setup of Drandok — almost like a halfway house between normality and criminality.

I accept that it's a big improvement on ignoring problems until they spiral out of control. It's better to know your potential enemies than believe they'll never pose a genuine threat. As we make our way along the narrow crevice, the walls glowing with light, I touch Conrad's hand to get his attention. We're on the way to watch Olin and Neve in action, waiting to see their response when we appear on the mountainside.

If Conrad's right and they appeared in Poridian Parlour to draw us here, he'll get the duel he's seeking. I'm just worried the two emotionless figures have got more than a friendly duel in mind, meaning our first trip to Drandok could be a memorable one.

Our Williynx stay close by, maintaining their tiny forms, as light appears at the far end of the narrow crevice: a sign we've almost reached our vantage point.

"Let's take it easy until we know more," I suggest, brushing my hand against Conrad's, getting his full attention.

He buttons his grey coat as if he's preparing for milder temperatures outside, ready to enter the taming range on the back of his trusted turquoise Williynx. "I'll only react to what I'm faced with."

"We don't want a battle on our first visit here," Lucy adds, adjusting the scarf around her neck.

We're all skilled Night Rangers, equally comfortable in the sky or on land, which doesn't mean the Silverbacks don't pose a problem. You normally encounter Silverbacks in battle, firing out a volley of defensive charms as your Williynx spins and shoots out blasts of ice.

As this *isn't* a battle, it's not going to be a straightforward case of storming towards the enemy because, in theory, there *isn't* an enemy ... just two silent soldiers with an axe to grind.

"We can watch the taming process from the mountain range," Orgev explains, stroking his beard again as if he's pondering something.

It looks like we're not the only ones who think Odin and Neve are shifty characters.

"It will give you a greater insight into how we use curses to test each Domitus," Orgev continues.

"So, the curses don't affect the creatures at all?" Lucy queries.

"Only to contain, leading to a slow submission. Remember, dark magic has a hypnotic effect on underworld creatures."

"And these vantage points help you to monitor how the curses are applied," Conrad adds, looking out over the mountain range framing the taming space, beginning to understand the intricacies of the process. As we join the crowds lining the mountain side, I keep my eyes on Odin and Neve who hover in the sky close by.

"Much will be revealed with your arrival," Orgev adds, "including the extent of their grudge."

I feel Laieya fluttering by my shoulder, struggling to maintain her minuscule form at the sight of the Riadek nearby: an old enemy from times gone by. It won't be long before the taming display begins ... the unchained Silverback below stretching its vast, armoured wings, attempting to regain enough strength to rise into the skies.

Conrad keeps the two emotionless Domitus in his sights. With our knowledge of Drandok improved, we now know where suspicion lies so wait for the right time to strike. As the weakened Silverback rises into the air, crashing into the mountain walls before regaining its sense of flight, the first wisp of black smoke appears from the hands of Odin and Neve: a Niavak curse creeping towards the ascending Silverback.

The cursed smoke circles around them, reminding me of matadors taming bulls. According to Orgev, the Niavak curse is only used to bring about submission. The question now is how much Odin and Neve enjoy the dark power at their disposal — the very reason curses are part of the taming ritual: to reveal soldiers whose scars have tipped them over the edge.

The two Domitus continue to circle on their armoured creatures, controlling the flight path of the weakened Silverback who falters at the sight of the black smoke. With the crowds looking on, monitoring every move, I step closer to Conrad who has edged away from the group, his turquoise Williynx shape-shifting into a slightly bigger form.

As Odin and Neve close in on the Silverback closer to us, they veer towards the mountain side, their Riadek's wings spiking as they fly past us: as clear sign they have an axe to grind. Conrad doesn't need any more encouragement, whistling for Erivan to reform in all his majesty. I do the same, calling Laieya into action. Less than a minute later all four Williynx are circling in the sky, ready for us to free fall into action.

There's no other way of attaching ourselves to our feathered companions so we jump off the mountainside ... the gasp from the crowds reaching us as we do. Free falling is one of the first tricks you learn as a Night Ranger, allowing for a dramatic introduction to battle.

We spin through the air on the back of our Williynx, avoiding the cursed smoke as we reach a higher vantage point, ready for the duel I knew was coming.

"Stay close together," Conrad says, "and keep an eye on the trail of smoke."

Odin and Neve rise higher in the sky, riding on either side of the weakened Riadek, a string of smoke running from their hands towards the creature's body.

"Once we close in, we'll know what their problem is," I add, readying my hand to release a defensive charm.

The S.P.M.A. hasn't exactly authorised this duel but, at the same time, it fits into their assessment of soldiers arousing suspicion. Like the use of the curses, the duel will draw out buried resentments, putting Odin and Neve on a path to redemption or punishment.

"Looks fairly harmless so far," Noah states as we rise higher, moments before the weakened Silverback's wings close and it falls from the sky.

"Normal formation!" Conrad shouts over the stricken Silverback's roar, and we form a circle to prepare for the colossal, armoured beast falling at speed.

It only takes a glance in the direction of Odin and Neve to know this is no accident, but we can take care of them later. Right now, there's a massive creature about to crash down on us so the force field charm is enacted ... a collective shout of 'FORA' generating an invisible blanket of protection, powerful enough to halt the Silverback's fall.

With the Fora charm doing its job, the Weveris charm is generated to add protective cover for our faces ... black webs over our noses and mouths as the wisps of cursed smoke stretch through the air, still under the command of the two Domitus who look on.

It's obvious what happens next ... the Niavak curse will close in, causing the Silverback to jolt into action, fear igniting into flight ... which is when we'll be faced with huge, armoured wings spiking into action. One strike of those wings is enough to sever a human body so I watch as the smoke closes in, remembering Orgev's comment that curses aren't used against creatures, but to reveal the dark intentions of the damaged and deranged.

Odin and Neve haven't revealed enough yet, making sure their 'mistake' happened at a distance, so it's time for a little surprise of our own: my favourite fire charm igniting the stricken Silverback into action. The fire lights up the Fora charm which continues to offer a protective blanket for us. I don't need to look at Conrad, Lucy and Noah to establish the plan because whenever there's fire, there's fury.

With the fire covering the Fora charm, the Riadek roars to life, bursting upwards once more ... only this time we use ice to freeze the cursed smoke ... leaving Odin and Neve to work out a Plan B before a revitalised beast rips them to shreds.

We need a safe place to watch the final phase from, whispering instructions to our Williynx who adapt smaller forms once more, using their claws to perch on the mountain face, slightly below the crowds looking on with interest.

"Don't you think we should help?" Lucy poses as the Riadek releases a colossal roar, a volley of defensive charms from Odin and Neve bouncing off its armour.

"They'll either tame it or lose control," I say, hovering in mid-air alongside my three allies, using my love of fire to add some spice to proceedings.

"They're going to get ripped to shreds," Noah adds, cringing as the two shifty Domitus dart through the skies, sending out ineffective showers of light and energy that do nothing to stop the beast on their tail.

"They're supposed to be creature tamers, aren't they?" Conrad adds, offering me a satisfying smile, "so let's find out what they're made of. They wanted this duel, after all."

It turns out that what Odin and Neve are made of is hollow courage, struggling to control the erratic flight of the Silverbacks they ride on. They dart at different angles to avoid their pursuers spiked, armoured wings, kicking hard to control their flight path as they whip out a fire charm of their own ... but it has no effect ... the velocity of the free Riadek too great to be stopped by clouds of fire.

As the crowds look on from the mountainside, the first mistake happens as the roaring Riadek crashes into Odin who falls from his weakened creature, enacting the flight charm to halt his fall. A single flower appears above his hand — the stem wrapping around his wrist as the flower spins in a propellor motion, easing him onto the ground.

He's an open target now, and with Neve using an invisibility charm to hide her fall only Odin remains in danger. Why he hasn't thought of making himself invisible is a puzzle, probably because he's caught in a scenario he didn't expect. He has to tame or be tamed, I realise, the entire principle that Drandok is founded on: the assessment of broken soldiers and the extent to which their minds have been darkened by battle.

Battle is the very thing Odin's faced with now, looking up to see the roaring Silverback closing in with another chained creature occupying the taming range below. Serious injury won't be allowed, obviously, but every move a Domitus makes in Drandok marks their future, and Odin's future doesn't look too bright at the moment.

If he doesn't find a way to tame the beast, he's proven himself unfit for duty, having already 'lost control' of the Riadek in the skies: a sneaky way of targeting us. It's a pity he didn't think of the consequences of tempting four Night Rangers to Drandok, knowing full well that two of them are already war veterans.

"I bet you any money he quits, leaving us to rescue him," Noah says as he rubs his companion's fire-red feathers.

"How much?" Conrad challenges, loving a bit of competition.

"Half the money I lost yesterday, thinking you wouldn't sing: a thousand Kyals to see who's right."

"You're on," Conrad replies with a confident smile as we get comfortable, ready to find out what Odin Blin is made of.

18

A SHOWER OF ICE

The expected bubble of light appears around Odin as the Riadek roars towards him, the activation of the Velinis charm likely to offer only temporary protection from a ferocious beast: Odin's going to need a lot more than this to escape unscathed.

The four of us perch on our Williynx on the mountain ridge, ready to intervene if necessary. The job of a Night Ranger is to keep the peace, after all, so we can't just sit back and watch a comrade come to harm, even if he is a potential malev in the making.

As the Silverback crashes into the ruby-red bubble of protection surrounding Odin, our Williynx squawk in an instinctive desire to intervene, but we whisper reassurances to them, rubbing their feathered coats to keep them calm. Although beautiful to look at, Williynx can be as fierce as any underworld creature, including the brutal beast that turns in flight, opening its armoured wings to smash into Odin's fragile defences.

The taming range has been cleared on the ground below — chained Silverbacks returned to their cells at the sight of potential carnage above. I'm fairly sure Odin's current predicament isn't in the training manual. All eyes are on us now as the ruby-red Velinis charm cracks, leaving Odin increasingly vulnerable to the vicious creature who circles again, letting out a roar that reverberates around the mountains.

The Riadek could make its escape, of course, finally free of the chains of its captors, but underworld creatures are designed for cruelty so vengeance remains the aim: the target now scrambling to retrieve a Zombul from his jacket pocket. It's the very artefact Alice Aradel sought out to protect herself with: a small, silver object punctuated with holes at the top.

A Zombul is able to release any creature small enough to explode from it ... the vampiric Ameedis bursting into life now swarming the Silverback as it closes in. The vicious, black birds have no impact on the creature, bouncing off its armour as they try to find flesh to sink their teeth into.

"This is getting out of hand," Lucy says, her slight figure tensing in mild frustration.

I know what she's thinking; we didn't sign up to observe cruelty so I echo her sentiments, adding, "Time to move in."

"What about the bet?" Noah asks, deciding not to pursue the point as Lucy glares at him.

"We're still on duty, remember," Lucy adds defiantly, "and Night Rangers *protect*."

With the crowds watching from above, lining the perch framing the triangular taming range, I catch a glimpse of Orgev's face — the muscle-bound, bearded Domitus who's provided clarity on the purpose of curses. His frown suggests his own suspicions, studying a group who arrived to get answers and are now raising doubts.

"We go as the Silverback spins into action," Conrad says,

rotating his neck slowly. "Fine ice bullets aimed at its throat ... enough to stun but not seriously wound ... no unnecessary cruelty."

With that, we prepare to take flight once more, knowing our timing has to be precise to counter the Riadek's roaring approach.

"*Now*," I say, signalling a co-ordinated return to action, flying low towards a stranded Odin who hovers in mid-air, courtesy of a flight charm which has turned out to be a poor choice. It limits his movements, placing him in a no-man's-land beneath the threat in the sky and potential danger below. It seems he's better at taming than fighting, so we move in to do our duty: the protection of comrades at all costs.

"A sheet of ice above Odin, protecting him from the Riadek's wings," Conrad instructs, "then ice bullets at the Silverback's throat to quell the danger."

We're in position seconds later ... a line of colour about to decorate the taming range with sheets of ice. A gentle whisper releases the first sheet of ice, stretching across the triangular space hidden in the mountains ... reaching Odin's stranded figure just in time. The enormous. armoured wings lashing out only to smash into the ice which shatters on impact.

It's enough to reset the Silverback, causing it to spin away with a roar of fury. As it turns, the second phase of the plan begins — ice bullets to the only vulnerable part of its body: the throat. Bullets fly through the air, arcing and looping towards their target ... some striking the armour to cause the necessary distraction while others hit home ... causing the Riadek to tilt in pain ... the spikes of steel decorating its wings closing in the first sign of weakness.

"*Now*, Guppy," Lucy says, gesturing towards Odin who's now struggling to control the vampiric birds he's released.

The Zombul controls whatever you release, but you have to *keep* control which is hard to do when you're suspended in the sky by a flight charm. The propellor-motion of the flower attached to Odin's hand is slowing — only a few petals remaining as a consequence of the Riadek's attack.

I stay low on Laieya as my trusted, powder-blue Williynx spins through shattered ice that flies in every direction. Odin is the target now, hanging onto the disintegrating flower as the vampiric Ameedis begin to turn on him, realising they're no longer under his control.

Thankfully, I get some help from the crowds looking on from above — streaks of multi-coloured light followed by a cry of 'DISINERIS', the disintegration charm exploding the Ameedis out of existence.

Now, it's just Odin to rescue before he falls to the earth. He's injured, probably from the vampiric birds he lost control of, meaning he's going to struggle to break his fall which starts seconds later. I pat Laieya into action, my feathered friend accelerating towards the grey soil ... in pursuit of a questionable comrade whose battle scars have darkened his spirit.

As Conrad, Noah and Lucy keep the injured Silverback occupied, using a Promesiun charm to restrict its flight, I feel the cold wind on my face as I reach out to grab Odin's flailing arm. He resists initially, turning to look at me as he's falling, the grimace a sign of his ingrained bitterness.

Whatever his issues, he's still a Society soldier so I do what's necessary, using the Fixilia charm to limit his ability to move: a charm causing terrible pain once you're frozen to the spot. He's even angrier now but I'm not interested in his bruised ego; he's close to smashing in to the ground so I spin underneath him, whipping out strings of light that wrap around his restricted figure.

The topaz-blue light of the Promesiun charm attaches him to my Williynx inches from the ground. We rise again ... Odin in front of me so I can keep an eye on him, the emotionless soldier of the Domitus clan grimacing every time he moves.

He's been humbled in public view — his bitter spirit exposed in the 'accidental' release of the Silverback he was supposed to be taming. The 'accident' was aimed at us, meaning Odin's time in Drandok is about to come to an end.

With Conrad, Noah and Lucy offering their own version of creature taming — bringing the injured Riadek to a submissive pause on the grey soil of the taming range — I rise towards Orgev who's clapping with the rest of the crowd, offering me a smile as I reach him. A final spin turns Odin over to Orgev: the concluding touch to an eventful evening.

As night falls, we sit in a circle around an array of food that's handed around the group. I initially wonder why we're sitting on the floor but decide not to ask. After all, Drandok is an unusual place in a lot of ways, not least because of the creatures resting in the cells below us. A rough guess places us in the centre of the mountain hollow: a communal space where all are welcome.

From the numbers sat around the circle, I guess that less than half the residents are here — the other half deciding to stay in the small space they call home, still struggling with troubling visions. Noah's never shy when it comes to food but receives a glare as he reaches for a bowl.

Lucy explains the ritual of waiting for the food to be handed to you, rolling her eyes at me afterwards. I still can't work out if Lucy's into Noah. She isn't the easiest person to read: an enigma wrapped in a small frame.

"So, what happens to Odin now?" Conrad asks, handing a bowl to me.

I'm not sure what's in the bowl, guessing it's seaweed. It doesn't look particularly appealing, but I run the risk of offending the Domitus if I don't eat it: the silent crew of soldiers studying me as I prepare to sample the food.

"A different form of rehabilitation," Orgev replies, sipping from a large clay cup.

"Sad Souls?" I ask, knowing what's waiting for Odin there: a transformation from legend to Melackin. Melackin are ex-members of the S.P.M.A., reduced to shadows of their former self via a combination of remedies administered by the Ulux: the ageing giants who inhabit Sad Souls.

My mum received this very treatment, living as a Melackin now in the twisted building beyond Society Sphere. It's the price you pay for minor betrayals, like the 'accidental' release of the Silverback Odin and Neve were supposed to be taming, hoping the creature would carry out their desired vengeance. According to Orgev, they blame Conrad and me for the death of their relatives in war, raising questions of loyalty.

If Odin and Neve's relatives caught our fire, they put themselves on that path. The principles of the S.P.M.A. are centred around peace, after all, retaliation only authorised in the face of a threat. It's a simple principle I live by: peace unless danger needs to be dealt with — the current danger being Odin and Neve Blin.

"Neve has already left Drandok," Orgev adds, "using the

Invisilis charm to avoid detection. We have ways of tracking her; sleeping soldiers are already on the move."

"Where's she likely to go?" Noah asks, accepting a bowl of glittering soup.

"To more remote places beyond The Society Sphere, staying hidden as long as possible. The Royisin Heights is the likely location. Neve won't surrender easily, preferring death in battle to a life imprisoned in The Velynx?"

"And what about Odin?" I ask. "Is he likely to surrender easily?"

"Time will tell," Orgev replies, studying the glittering walls. "Drandok isn't a prison, after all, meaning recuperating soldiers can come and go as they please."

"Even after Odin tried to set the Silverback on us?" Lucy challenges, sipping from the cup she's handed: Jysyn Juice, hopefully.

"He knows the fate that awaits him, Lucy. It's for Odin to accept it or resist."

"And if he resists?" Conrad prompts.

"Then a journey to Quibbs Causeway will be his fate, where the Mantzils await — more devastating than the Silverbacks and ready to unhinge his mind."

"Is Neve on a Silverback or on foot?" I ask.

"On foot," comes the reply from the eldest of the bearded soldiers, sitting opposite me in the circle of gathered soldiers. "Her recent habit of taking her creature out of Drandok was her first mistake.

The Shallows attract mild-mannered witches and wizards — the reason Odin and Neve risked arriving on their Silverbacks. Other places are not so welcoming. She'll survive on her wits now until we catch up with her."

"We can always help," Conrad suggests, the tension in

his body easing as knowledge of Odin and Neve's fate comes to light.

Unfortunately for them, they've picked the wrong fight: a fight we're going to bring to their door. The night is young and Neve couldn't have got far on foot. My instincts tell me Odin will soon follow, taking his chances in the vast spaces beyond The Society Sphere.

We've saved his life once which doesn't mean we will again. Not that we're out to kill either of them, but Society rules are clear: betrayal puts you on the path of rehabilitation or imprisonment — so the stage is set for another meeting with the two Domitus who brought a fight to their door.

19

NIGHT VISIONS

The stars come out as we leave Drandok ... a picture of serenity which contrasts with the roaring thunder we heard on our arrival. The roars were from the chained Riadek who, it seemed, were being tamed by curses. We know this isn't the case now — the cursed smoke more to test how damaged the recuperating soldiers are: soldiers known as the Domitus.

Two of the Domitus have been exposed as harbouring dangerous levels of resentment: Odin and Neve Blin who won't be able to hide from their fate for too long. Neve is on the run, possibly making her way to The Royisin Heights, while Odin is holed up in the mountains of Drandok, or at least that's the theory.

As Orgev explained, Drandok is a place where shell-shocked soldiers choose to come to. They can choose to stay or to leave — exits only forced when intentions are questionable. My money's on Odin going the same way as Neve, making a quick escape in fear of a Society army descending on Drandok to drag him to Quibbs Causeway.

That's not going to happen, though, because the 'accident' of losing control of the Silverback isn't enough for a stay in The Velynx: the faculty for bad things and bad people. Instead, we've got to be patient, saying our goodbyes to Orgev and his bearded crew as we rise into the sky on our Williynx: a decision to be made on where the night leads us next.

As we rise higher towards the stars, our figures in silhouette, Conrad stays close to me — the grey overcoat and white T-shirt marked by our little drama in the taming range. I prefer it when he's less preoccupied with Society business, the look of mischief returning to his eyes.

"So, The Royisin Heights or back to The Singing Quarter?" Conrad asks, his smile suggesting he's leaning more towards romance than reconnaissance.

We can track down Odin and Neve another day — a group of sleeping soldiers already on their tracks, as Orgev explained, so I'm also leaning towards a return to The Singing Quarter, looking forward to more fun in Rebel's Rest — Noah's singing only part of the entertainment. We all know what Noah's going to choose, already clearing his throat to see if he can hit the notes that evade him.

"Back to The Singing Quarter, obviously," Noah replies, brushing the fringe away from his eyes. "I need to get my solo in before closing time."

Closing time is whenever the Tallis family who run Rebel's Rest have had enough of the regulars, Zoe Tallis charming the stragglers out of the doors, Periums returning Society folk to their dwellings.

"What's the song going to be this time?" Lucy asks as her yellow Williynx glides silently through the night sky.

"I'm thinking *Rebel Blues*," Noah says before he blasts out the first few lines. "Evening's falling / I'm here all alone / Feel rain coming / Can't make it on my own ..."

It's a depressing song about being rejected and ignored — perfect for Noah's obsession with Zoe Tallis — which doesn't stop us enjoying it, adding our little rhythm between each line. Noah doesn't need encouragement: a natural comedian with a gift for the ridiculous. The song takes the edge off an eventful evening, involving taming Silverbacks and saving a shifty Domitus: all in a night's work for a Night Ranger.

Noah adds a little spin on the back of his Williynx, getting more into the song at the most depressing part. "How could you leave me broken? / Hopeless, bitter and blue / But here I am still hoping / That there's a chance for me and you ..."

To be honest, I wish Zoe Tallis would just go on a date with Noah. Then again, that might actually make him *worse*, babbling on about her until one of us has to use the Vyoxal charm to shut him up. The Vyoxal charm restricts your vocal cords, removing the ability to speak. It's the one charm I love using above ground, mainly for old school friends I can't stand.

Conrad, Lucy and I add the single-line chorus. "*Chance for me and you,*" we sing together, Conrad dragging out the 'you' part as he flies higher, arms spread out as he hits the notes Noah never quite can.

I love his unpredictability, hating public displays unless he's in trusted company. High up in the night sky above Drandok, he can be as ridiculous as any teenage boy, enjoying the freedom of adolescence, temporarily unburdened by Society business.

As I watch him belt out the chorus one more time,

drawing fits of laughter from Noah and Lucy, I remember the first time I met Conrad — a timid boy standing on the ground floor of The Cendryll lost in grief. He hadn't found himself then, discovering his gift for flight on his first trip to Gilweean.

He's the youngest leader of the sky-rider army in the Society's history, and the boy I love completely rides alongside Noah as the comical performance comes to a close — our friendship framed by a starlit sky on a night that's brought clarity to the purpose of a hidden few.

With other Society soldiers on the trail of Odin and Neve, we can rest for now, knowing our part in their arrest can be put on hold, meaning we can enjoy the strange silence that falls over Drandok — the Riadek resting in their dark cells and our Williynx enjoying the freedom of an untroubled sky. If we race, we'll get back to Rebel's Rest in time for last orders.

~

WE APPEAR THROUGH A PERIUM IN THE SKY ACCESSIBLE TO our feathered companions, gliding above the quiet evening streets. The sight of groups of witches and wizards exiting the building suggests it's near to closing time so we descend quickly, dismounting from our Williynx who bid us good evening with a parting squawk.

"Remember, you lost the bet," Noah says to Conrad as we enter the noise of Rebel's Rest.

"How did I lose the bet?" Conrad challenges, brushing Drandok dust off his grey jeans.

"We bet that Odin would quit in the taming range, leaving us to rescue him."

"But he didn't quit; he got *stuck*."

Noah turns to Lucy and me, gesturing for support.

"He was hanging in mid-air as the Silverback closed in on him," Lucy adds, shrugging her shoulders. "I wouldn't call that quitting."

"But we had to *rescue* him," Noah says, realising he's about to lose *another* thousand Kyals, having recently lost money to Lucy and me when Conrad suddenly burst into song.

"Rescuing him only if he *quit* was the bet," Conrad counters with a smile, holding out his hand for payment. "Odin didn't quit so pay up, unless you don't honour your bets, of course."

Noah's face clouds at this suggestion, questioning the honour of any Society soldier the easiest way to trigger a response.

"Jysyn Juice on you," Noah says grudgingly as he hands Conrad the bag of Kyals: Society money that comes in handy in magical establishments.

~

NOAH'S FACE LIGHTS UP AT THE SIGHT OF ZOE TALLIS BEHIND the bar, untroubled by the groups that normally occupy her time and attention.

"Perfect timing," Lucy whispers encouragingly, nudging Noah towards the bar. "Remember, cool, calm and collected and *don't sing*."

I suppress a giggle, walking to the empty table closest to the bar, providing a view of the busy evening streets — full of colour and sound as Society members joke and laugh, ambling past closed shops in a world hidden from above-ground eyes.

Soon, they will use portable Periums to return them to

faculties or above-ground dwellings. It's always fun to sit and watch as sparks of light fill the evening streets, forming into arches of colour for witches and wizards to vanish through.

I SIT BETWEEN CONRAD AND LUCY IN THE EMPTYING RESTING rooms of Rebel's Rest, secretly wishing Noah good luck with Zoe Tallis. Zoe's friendly with all the regulars, her wit and wisdom making her aware of those with hopes for romance. She's never given Noah any obvious signs which hasn't put him off yet, so I divide my attention between the first portable Periums appearing on the streets outside, and Noah trying to work a different type of magic at the bar.

"That's a good sign," Conrad says at the sight of Zoe laughing at something Noah's said.

"The magic's happening, at last," Lucy adds with what I sense to be a glimmer of jealousy.

Is she into Noah, after all? If so, why's she secretive about it? Lucy's a mixture of prettiness and sarcasm: not the best combination when you're trying to win someone over. Her interactions with Noah are a mixture of reassurances and friendly put downs, which would make *anybody* wonder.

Not that I'm an expert in any way. I hardly noticed boys until Conrad, but there are ways of showing you like someone, making me wonder why Lucy *encouraged* Noah to talk to Zoe if she likes him?

Conrad nudges me, whispering, "It's all an act."

He gestures to Lucy — an unmistakable cloud of jealousy crossing her face as Zoe laughs again. Lucy *does* like Noah so it's time for me to work some magic of my own, wondering how I can get my hands on some Telynin (truth serum) which will *definitely* do the trick.

There's obviously the issue of Lucy being tricked into telling Noah how she feels — the truth serum loosening her tongue — meaning if she realises she doesn't *love* him, we mess up Noah's chances with Zoe. I'm starting to think we should have stayed out beyond The Society Sphere, heading to The Royisin Heights to track Neve down.

Conrad nudges me again, recognising the introspection I sometimes get lost in. "They'll work it out," he whispers, keeping his eye on Noah's nervous interactions at the bar.

He's got more faith than I have in Lucy ever expressing how she feels, but he's right — it's up to them to work it out. Although, this won't stop me thinking about how we can *help*. I mean, what's the benefit of magic if you can't add a little wonder to people's lives?

Noah finally returns with four glasses of Jysyn Juice and a Parasil: a self-refilling glass container. The Parasil suggests Zoe's not planning to close anytime soon, meaning we'll soon have Rebel's Rest to ourselves: a nice reward for an eventful evening.

"So ...?" I ask, curious at the grin on Noah's face.

"I've got a *date*," he whispers, sipping his Jysyn Juice with a shaking hand. "Tomorrow night in The Winter Quarter."

"*No way*," Lucy responds with a little too much intensity. "You've got a date with *Zoe Tallis* ...?"

"Yep," Noah says, checking himself over in the window. His chinos, grey T-shirt and matching waistcoat are fairly unmarked after our skirmish in Drandok. "Seven p.m. tomorrow which means no night ranging for me."

"Good man," Conrad says, patting Noah on the back. "You've finally worn her down."

"Very funny," Noah replies, clearly getting stressed at the

idea of the date. "So, what do I wear?" he asks, getting only a shrug from me.

"*Come on,*" he prompts to Lucy and me, "I need a *woman's* touch."

"You'll have that tomorrow night," Lucy replies with her usual sarcasm but she can't hide the envy, causing her more pain than she realises.

"Seriously, guys, I need your help. *What do I wear?* And where do I book a table?"

"Merrymopes definitely," Conrad suggests.

Merrymopes is Conrad's favourite place — the magical milkshake and ice cream parlour in Founders' Quad. I love it too, but I'm not sure it's going to be Zoe's idea of a first date.

"I'd say somewhere more sophisticated," I suggest.

"Like where?"

"Wimples ...?" I reply, getting the expected laugh from Conrad and Lucy.

Noah doesn't find the idea of date in a sweetshop so funny.

"You're not helping, Guppy."

"Velerin's," Lucy suggests. "It's the classiest restaurant in The Winter Quarter. You'll impress Zoe if you take her there. It's also near The Sinking Bridge where couples go on first dates, hoping to share their first kiss."

Noah turns to Lucy, surprised by her attention to detail. "Thanks, Lucy; that really helps."

"Any time," Lucy replies with a smile that hides her true feelings.

"Can you pay in Kyals at Velerin's?" Noah asks, glancing at the sight of a wizard vanishing through a portable Perium outside.

Conrad takes the bag of Kyals from his Keepeasy. "Here,"

he says, handing Noah the bag of Kyals back. "A first date's more important than a bet."

With that, we raise our glasses in celebration of Noah's success with Zoe Tallis — the barmaid who watches us clink our glasses with a strange smile.

20

ROMANCE & REFLECTIONS

With Noah getting ready for his date and sleeping soldiers on the tail of Neve Blin, Conrad and I decide to spend the early evening in The Cendryll. We sit in my bedroom on the fourth floor, something that's allowed in the daytime with strict orders for Conrad to be in his own room or elsewhere before nightfall.

Although we're Night Rangers, eighteen is still the magical number for official wizarding status, meaning we've been accepted but are still treated like kids in some regards. Not that this is a big deal as there are plenty of places where our romance can thrive, the top floor of The Weary Winzer our favoured spot at present.

No-one really goes there and an Invisilis charm keeps us hidden from anyone using surveillance devices to see what we're up to. A girl needs her privacy, after all. For now, though, the romance in question is Noah's date with the girl he's been chasing forever: Zoe Tallis.

I'm still in shock that Zoe's agreed to go on a date with Noah. Not because I think she's out of his league; it's more that she's always seemed *separate* ... as if she enjoys the attention of the regulars in Rebel's Rest, but no more than that. The only niggling doubt I have is linked to the strange smile she had on her face, watching us celebrate Noah's success last night in Rebel's Rest.

I just hope she's not stringing him along, only giving him the date to stop his endless pursuit of her. It will crush Noah if she's building his hopes up, but Zoe doesn't strike me as a cruel person so I sit with Conrad on my bed, studying the Panorilum that hovers in the middle of the room: the big piece of parchment paper that acts as one of the Society's surveillance devices.

The large, moving illustration of Society Square focused in on Velerin's: the location of the date. Conrad's never liked spying on people who aren't enemies, saying it's weird to check on friends and comrades. I think it's normal but I'm a pretty nosy person, so we leave Noah and Zoe in peace, preparing for a date we'll probably never hear the end of.

"I bet Lucy's watching their every move," I say, sitting cross-legged on my bed with Churchill perched on the end.

Churchill is Kaira's cat, and I've offered to look after him while Kaira's on her travels. He's gentle and doesn't require a lot of fuss, just wanting company like all of us. I tap the bed to invite Churchill over — an invitation he accepts, settling in my lap.

"Probably," Conrad replies in reference to Lucy struggling with her feelings for Noah, whatever they are. "We should help her to take her mind off the date."

"What have you got in mind?"

"Some night ranging ... maybe a trip to The Royisin Heights."

"To track Neve, you mean?"

Conrad strokes Churchill before adding, "We're probably going to have to, anyway, helping us to explain how we got into a firefight with her in Drandok. I'm sure Casper will know if she's holed up in The Royisin Heights."

"Can't we leave that until tomorrow night?" I suggest. "I'd rather watch how the date goes."

"Which is a bit weird."

"Why?"

"Watching our friend on his first date with the girl he's wanted for ages ...?"

"It's *encouragement*," I suggest in an unconvincing tone.

"It's prying in personal business."

"And a trip to The Royisin Heights is another trek beyond The Society Sphere," I reply. "A job other sleeping soldiers are taking care of."

"Don't you want to know where Neve is hiding? And if Odin's left Drandok?"

"Yes, I want to know, but we can use the Panorilum to find that out, can't we."

"It's not the same as visiting, seeing them with our own eyes."

It's obvious Conrad doesn't want to watch the date, maybe sharing my concern that Zoe's potentially stringing Noah along. If he *is* worried about this, he obviously won't want to see his friend humiliated, so I make him a deal.

"Okay, we wait for Noah and Zoe to get to Velerin's, just so we know he hasn't been let down, and then we contact Lucy and head to The Royisin Heights. That way, we help both our friends."

"Deal," Conrad says, grabbing my waist as we fall onto the bed laughing, conscious that Society eyes might be on us. We know the limits of 'decorum' as Society elders like to put it, deciding to push the edge of those limits, getting lost in one another until another date begins.

THE SIGHT OF NOAH APPEARING OUTSIDE VELERIN'S RETURNS our attention to the Panorilum hovering in the bedroom. The restaurant is in the magical part of The Winter Quarter, decorated by snow that falls all year round.

There's nothing like the Society anywhere else in the world, and you can never get tired of the endless wonders it offers. Velerin's is another wonder: a globe-shaped building formed of glass and steel, rotating anti-clockwise on the hour. The snow adds a decorative touch to the building, drawing couples seeking a romantic backdrop to their evening.

The colourful glow is one of the best things about Velerin's, the lighting inside coming from the Spintz charms hovering above each table, formed in the shape of a chandelier in the colour of the diners' penchants. When it rotates on the hour, you get a glimpse of the people inside — couples mainly and the odd family, the children absorbed by a winter wonderland of colour.

It's not the sort of place you drop into and you're encouraged to dress up for the occasion, something Noah's clearly taken to heart. He's abandoned his chino and waistcoat look for a purple suit decorated by a gold pocket chain. He's also got some gel in his hair from the way his fringe spikes up into a quiff. I'm not sure about the hair gel but he looks the part. All we're waiting for now is the arrival of Zoe Tallis.

I start to get nervous when the minutes pass, the moving illustration on the Panorilum offering no clues to Zoe's whereabouts until she appears out of nowhere, using a Cympgus to add a touch of drama to her arrival. The girl's got style, that's for sure, stepping through the portable Perium to the delight of Noah.

Zoe's drawn to a more classic look like the dress and coat she's wearing now, looking like she belongs in a 1920s movie. The Winter Quarter helps with the backdrop, Edwardian buildings stretching high to add to the image of romance Noah and Zoe are doing their best to maintain.

"They look good," I say to Conrad who smiles at the sight of Noah offering Zoe flowers.

"A nice touch," he comments as they head for Velerin's, the snow swirling around them.

With Velerin's rotating slowly in the snow, offering a glimpse of romantic meals within, Noah maintains his gentlemanly rhythm, opening the door for Zoe who lifts her dress as she steps in, waiting inside to be met by an equally elegant woman who takes them to their table on the top floor.

The choice of table was also Lucy's idea, a strange attention to detail from a girl who harbours certain feelings for Noah, but that's a puzzle for another day. For now, we've agreed to keep Lucy company to take her mind off the date: a bit of night ranging and a trip to The Royisin Heights.

As Noah and Zoe reach their table, Conrad utters 'Undilum' to deactivate the Panorilum — the large piece of parchment folding of its own accord, returning to the little book its hidden within when not in use. Reaching out for the book as it spins in mid-air, I return it to my Keepeasy stitched into my black, leather trousers, readying myself for another journey beyond The Society Sphere.

I'd rather stay here with Conrad, keeping Kaira's cat company, but we've promised to spend time with Lucy: a friend and comrade who just might need a distraction this evening. The Royisin Heights will give her that — a group of hills that stretch upwards and outwards, dotted with mounds of earth where the most reclusive members inhabit, almost monkish in their existence.

I always wondered why anyone would choose to stay in Drandok, but that's clearer now: a rehab centre for ravaged soldiers trying to keep a grip on their minds. The Royisin Heights is more straightforward: a place for witches and wizards wanting no part of modern Society life.

Lots of realms in the S.P.M.A. choose to have no ties to the above-ground world, having no interest in rubbing shoulders with the unmagical masses. The Royisin Heights takes this to the extreme, though, as if the people that stay up there have checked out of life altogether.

The large mounds of soil frame the homes inside — homes that are much bigger than the mounds suggest, the benefits of magic being the one thing the inhabitants haven't abandoned. Part of me wonders if it's the place Alice Aradel used as a hideout once her life as the evening witch disintegrated. If it is, we're likely to find more interesting characters hiding up there, looking to be left alone for different reasons.

The majority are left alone, of course, the Society respecting all ways of living that don't threaten its existence. Odin and Neve don't pose a real threat, but choices have consequences. Their choice of releasing a Silverback in our direction in Drandok has limited their future to two options: rehabilitation or judgement.

I've got the feeling they aren't going to accept either choice, meaning we'll soon meet again in unfriendly circumstances.

"Do you think Zoe really likes Noah?" I ask Conrad as we get ready to leave, returning to the ground floor where our Williynx will soon appear.

"It's hard to say," Conrad replies, taking a black T-shirt from my wardrobe.

I have a habit of borrowing his clothes which doesn't bother him — until he can't find them, that is. As he changes T-shirts, his toned torso marked by the scar running diagonally across his body, I feel a touch of sympathy for Lucy, not knowing how I can help without offending either friend.

If I try to help Lucy, she could brush off my good intentions with a flat out denial or, worse, anger at my prying nature. If I ask Conrad to mention it to Noah, he'll probably refuse. Even if Conrad *does* mention it, Noah might wonder why he's bringing it up when he's finally got a chance with Zoe.

The most obvious reason for *not* bringing it up is not knowing how Noah feels about Lucy. They're close but that doesn't necessarily mean anything, considering we're a group of Night Rangers who spend a lot of time together. You *have* to be close because you're entering shady situations, relying on your comrades for back up.

Conrad gives me a hug, kissing me on my lips.

"You're overthinking things," he says, always knowing when I'm preoccupied. "Let Noah enjoy his date and leave Lucy to work things out. If she doesn't know *what* she feels, anything we do to help will almost certainly backfire."

"But, they'd be good together."

"We don't know that, Guppy, so let's not create an imagined romance which could mess up a friendship."

"We were friends first."

"True, but I knew you secretly loved me."

I pinch his waist. "You're getting a bit too confident. It must be all the attention you're getting from Lorena in The Chattering Tap."

"Lorena flirts with everyone."

"Especially you."

"I'm just a likeable guy," Conrad teases with a smile that always wins me over.

"You're a cocky guy."

"And you're a beautiful girl."

I'm close to calling off our trip to The Royisin Heights, wondering if Lucy's better off left alone, working out her feelings as she watches Noah on his date. No doubt, she'll have a Panorilum or Follygrin to hand, so should we risk interrupting her fun when there's fun to be had here?

I keep my arms around Conrad's waist, moving in a slow dance in the bedroom, Churchill observing from the windowsill he's now perched on, wondering if we're ever going to leave.

21

THE ROYISIN HEIGHTS

We agree to meet Lucy in The Winter Quarter where she's decided to hang out for the evening (no need to guess why). We find her on the Sinking Bridge, looking down into the river with her yellow Williynx perched on the bridge alongside her, adopting a smaller form.

Lucy has used her penchant — a ring on the middle finger of her left hand — to illuminate the bridge in the colour of her penchant stone: a gentle citrine yellow lighting up the darkness. Lucy's enacting a Society ritual for couples on first dates.

The Sinking Bridge has a few layers of magic, including the ability to transport cars to other magical realms. Romantics like it because of the way it shimmers into life. Couples step onto it, placing their penchants on its wooden surface, watching as the bridge glows in the colour of their penchant stones, lighting up The Winter Quarter.

What couples *really* hope for, though, is the sight of the bridge spilling its colour onto the water below: the true mark of love, apparently. Noah and Zoe will have to wait and see if they can light up the bridge with their penchant stones.

The bridge is currently illuminated by a dull yellow light, reflecting Lucy's emotional state. Never one to show her feelings, her sullen posture on the bridge says it all. The fact she's chosen to meet us in The Winter Quarter is a sign of how much she's struggling with her feelings ... even more reason to *talk* about how she feels.

Maybe she views it as weakness, but mildly stalking a boy you secretly like when he's on his first date with another girl isn't particularly healthy.

"We get her into the sky as soon as possible," Conrad suggests as we walk past Velerin's, catching a glance of Noah and Zoe as the globe-shaped, glass restaurant spins anti-clockwise on the hour.

We've left it until eight p.m. to meet Lucy — my designs on staying in for the evening not quite going to plan. I got over my selfish desire to cuddle up with Conrad when I saw Lucy standing on the bridge alone, using my Follygrin to check on her whereabouts.

She's been standing on the bridge for over half an hour now, lost in her thoughts of what could have been, or something else she's not prepared to talk about. There's only so much you can do for friends when they don't want to help themselves, so we prepare to take to the skies, whistling to our Williynx as Conrad and I step onto The Sinking Bridge.

The old me would have 'acquired' one of the cars parked on the snow-covered streets, keen to drive over The Sinking Bridge before vanishing through it: a fun Perium leading to The Shallows. That's not our destination this evening, though, The Royisin Heights calling instead.

"Hey," Lucy says as we reach her.

Conrad gestures for me to engage in conversation,

tapping his hand on the bridge as Erivan perches alongside him, inspecting the water that glimmers below

"Ready to head to The Royisin Heights?" I ask Lucy who keeps her gaze on the water.

"A few more minutes," she replies, lifting the hood on her coat in the way she does when she's brooding on something.

I wonder if mentioning Noah is a good idea but decide against it. It would confirm if her sullen mood is linked to his date, but that's a fairly cruel way of testing a friend's emotional radar, so I decide to keep conversation casual. "Odin's left The Shallows like we thought he would."

"Where to?" Lucy asks, her pixie face studying the swirling water below.

"Don't know yet. He's using the Invisilis charm to stay hidden from prying eyes. Surveillance devices will pick him up soon enough. He'll make the same mistake Alice Aradel did, making an appearance when he's run out of places to hide."

"Yep," Conrad echoes, stroking Erivan as his feathered companion flaps its wings, rising from the bridge to inspect the still water below.

I then have an idea to cheer Lucy up, uttering 'Exhibius' to activate my penchant, watching as a soft blue light runs from my hand across the bridge, connecting with the yellow glow Lucy's created.

Conrad picks up on the idea, tapping his right hand to activate the ring on his forefinger ... a slow flood of tanzanite meeting our two colours until the bridge is lit up like a rainbow, drawing looks from witches and wizards occupying the snow-covered streets of The Winter Quarter.

We stand on the bridge a little while longer, allowing Lucy the time she needs to process whatever's going in her head. It only takes a few minutes for her to snap out of it, laughing as the three of us walk arm-in-arm across the bridge, mirroring the romantic gesture of couples who will soon be doing the same. I can tell she appreciates the moment: the enigmatic pixie girl struggling with the mysteries of the heart.

With a whistle, our Williynx are ready, rising off the bridge as they expand, a single feather released to add their own decoration. The feathers rest on the surface of the water, creating three strands of connected colour ... yellow, powder-blue and turquoise ... the final touch of magic before the night ranging begins once more.

"Apparently, we need to signal our arrival in The Royisin Heights," Conrad says as we rise into the air. "As long as we do, we'll be left to roam freely."

"Why do we need to signal our arrival?" Lucy asks.

"They're sort of recluses," I reply, "meaning they like to be left alone."

"Which means it's going to be hard to track Neve down," Lucy adds.

"Yep, but it's more a case of information gathering for now," I say as we bank left, the snow swirling around us. "We'll probably meet other Society soldiers on the way who can hopefully tell us more."

"But we're not bringing her in?"

Conrad shakes his head. "We find out where she's hiding and track her from there. Once we've got sight of her, we wait until she makes her first mistake, then the sleeping soldiers take care of the rest."

"Quibbs Causeway?" Lucy prompts.

"If she resists arrest, yep. An uncomfortable meeting with The Orium Circle if she doesn't."

"Well, let's make the most of things," I suggest, thinking

of another way to take Lucy's mind off Noah. "I'm still the fastest in the air from a dead start, so let's see if I've lost my touch."

Lucy adjusts her hood as she checks our positions, patting her Williynx to slow down. With a confident smile, she turns to Conrad adding, "No games or tricks allowed."

"What tricks?"

"Like suddenly swinging left and right, trying to knock us off because you're losing."

It's a bit of fun, leaving the question of love to be answered another day. Matters of the heart are no easier in the S.P.M.A. than anywhere else, the only difference being you've got *wonder* to snap you out of depressing moments. After all, what's more wonderful than flying through the sky on a majestic, colourful bird that can shape shift and blast ice ... snow falling on your face as you race through a winter wonderland.

~

THE ROYISIN HEIGHTS ARE SITUATED TO THE EAST OF Drandok — accessible by foot or air although Neve Blin hasn't got the luxury of arriving on a Silverback this time. The taming of these creatures happens exclusively in Drandok, and now Neve has exposed her hidden resentment, she no longer has the benefits of being a Domitus.

Orgev, our bearded guide in Drandok, believes The Royisin Heights is the most likely place to find Neve, the nature of the inhabitants offering the ideal conditions of privacy required for a potential malev.

As Conrad said, we're going to need to signal our arrival to be left to roam a place that stretches for miles, marked by mounds of earth, framing the dwelling places of the reclusive people who choose to live there. I'd go mad in a place like that, only the wind and sky for company when you choose to step outside.

It's a bit like Drandok in that it draws Society members who've chosen a separate existence, although the inhabitants of The Royisin Heights aren't broken, preferring isolation to Society duty in one of the many faculties and buildings making up the modern part of the S.P.M.A.

As the silhouette of the landscape comes into view, we ready our Spintz charms to signal our arrival — showers of multi-coloured light appearing in the night sky. I don't know if I expected figures to appear from the mounds of earth dotted through The Royisin Heights, but no figures appear so we touch down, keeping the Spintz charms active to light the way.

The darkness is the first surprising thing, resting like a blanket over the place where with no sound or visible signs of movement: the perfect hideout for shifty character like Neve Blin.

"Here," Lucy offers, handing me a vial of clear liquid: eye drops known as Crilliun to help you see in the dark.

I pass the vial to Conrad after administering the eye drops, blinking as a purple glow tints my vision: another magical touch in an infinite world of wonder. Wonder isn't how I'd describe this place, though, looking more like a burial site than a land of the living.

"A bit creepy out here," Lucy states, echoing my own thoughts.

It would be easy to get into a fire fight simply because you can't *see* anything, making it easy to over react if someone suddenly pops up out of nowhere. We're not here for another duel though, just to track down the lady who thought she'd got the better of us in Drandok: a mistake she's going to pay for.

"So, what's the plan?" Conrad asks, blinking as the Cril-liun eyedrops begin to work their magic.

"We just wander, I suppose," I reply, conscious that our Williynx have maintained their massive, majestic forms: a sign we need to be on our guard.

"A 'hello' would be nice," Conrad adds, unbuttoning his grey coat in readiness for sudden action, should it be needed.

I doubt it's going to be needed, judging from the *blank-ness* of the place — but looks can be deceiving so I ready a fire charm just in case, uttering 'Smekelin' to activate a circle of flames around me.

"That's a bit dramatic," Lucy says, glancing at me as we tread carefully across the silent landscape, decorated only by our Spintz charms and my fire.

"It's about the *only* dramatic thing here," I reply which leads Conrad to flash a streak of light into the air, triggering the Promesiun charm into action.

He's funny when he gets bored, always thinking of some-thing to add interest, and the circling string of tanzanite light adds another touch of drama to the blank landscape.

"Your turn," I say to Lucy with a smile, hoping she can use some magic to let off a bit of steam.

Lucy does me proud with a blast of water, the utterance of 'Levenan' causing a flood to surge from her hands. She adds the 'Iscillus' charm soon after, gently forming two arches of ice ahead of us — arches in the form of an enor-mous bridge, suggesting she's still got Noah on her mind.

With the ice arches dominating the landscape, we now have a touch of drama to pass the time, and I'm hoping we either find Neve quickly or get out of here before someone takes offence at the way we've decorated their home.

"It looks like we're in for a boring night," I say, seconds before the ice arches explode and a figure appears through the falling shards: a silent silhouette arriving to offer an unusual welcome.

22

A STRANGE WELCOME

As the final fragments of ice fall onto the ground, the figure steps closer, walking casually towards us to signal no active threat. I glimpse the face behind the long, greying hair ... a female face with intense, grey eyes. I'm struck by the woman's intensity, as if she's moving towards an object rather than a group of people.

It's the way she looks past us that's most off-putting, making me turn back to check there's no threat lurking behind us, but there's nothing but blank landscape and a dark, starless sky.

Something tells me conversation isn't what she's seeking so I stand alongside Conrad and Lucy, trying to work out our next move. This becomes apparent when she gestures for us to follow her, her long, greying hair lifting as she turns back the way she came ... her bare feet stepping onto the ice shards without drawing a trace of blood.

With our trusted Williynx hovering above, sniffing out potential threats hidden in the darkness, Conrad taps me on the arm.

"This is weird," Conrad whispers, keeping his Promesiun charm active, swirls of tanzanite light circling around his arms.

"She doesn't seem like the party type," Lucy quips, glancing around to make sure there aren't other silent silhouettes hovering in the darkness.

"So, do we follow or not?" I ask, feeling myself walking towards her before I get an answer.

"Maybe we should ask where she's taking us," Lucy suggests but I keep walking, wanting to find out more about this place, the silent figure and whether Neve is actually hiding out here or not. I mean, what's the worst the strange woman can do? Attack us? It's three against one and we're confident our powers unless, of course, she's drawing us into a cursed cavern hidden within the mound of earth she disappears into.

Sensing Conrad and Lucy aren't as keen to blindly following the stranger, I offer a thought. "We could still be on the bridge in The Winter Quarter or having a quiet night roaming Society Square. Instead, we're out in the middle of nowhere, tracking a person we're not sure is even here — so let's find out what we can and get out of here. At least we had the Domitus and Silverbacks to entertain us in Drandok."

"We don't need to go looking for trouble, Guppy," Conrad adds, picking up his pace to catch up with me.

"True, but trouble seems to find us either way. Come on, let's find out who the silent witch is."

WE REACH THE MOUND OF EARTH BUT SEE NO SIGN OF THE figure who waved us on, wondering what charm's required to enter. After placing our penchants on the outer edge of the mound, we try the 'Entrinius' incantation but nothing happens, making me wonder if we should just return to The Winter Quarter, checking in on Noah.

Will he get his long-hoped for kiss from Zoe or not? Is the date going well in Velerin's? Neither question really helps the current situation, and I doubt Lucy would thank me for taking us back there.

"Any ideas?" Conrad asks as we look around to see if the silent witch is evident in the darkness ahead, but there's nothing but our active charms and other mounds of earth dotting the landscape.

If my understanding of The Royisin Heights is right, each mound houses reclusive Society members who rarely leave their dwellings, which doesn't bode well for getting any assistance, finally arriving in a line of soil that runs down the side of the large mound ... forming around our feet and running up our bodies until it covers our penchants.

"Maybe we should give up on looking for Neve tonight," Conrad suggests, his impatience getting the better of him. "I'm not really in the mood to deal with another group of people who can't communicate without dragging us through places in silence."

"You sound like you didn't enjoy our little dance with the Silverbacks last night," I joke, giving into my natural curiosity to find out more. It's only a matter of time before the moving soil grants access or morphs into a dangerous creature: a typical night for a Night Ranger.

"I think she's trying to help us," Lucy suggests as the soil forms a rope between our penchants and the mound of earth, pulling us closer. Our feathered companions perch on the ropes of soil, fluttering their colourful wings as we approach the mound of earth.

"Really?" Conrad queries. "A woman appears out of nowhere, walking barefoot over ice fragments before vanishing back into the earth, and you think she's trying to help us?"

"It's *The Royisin Heights*, Conrad. The people are *recluses*, remember. What did you expect: a party?"

"We were actually having our own party in The Cendryll ..."

"Shut up, Conrad," I say, my stern look warning him not to rub in the fact we've got each other. Lucy's still hurting and taking out his impatience on her isn't fair or kind. "We've signed up for this, remember, ranging at night to keep the peace, so let's get on with it and get out of here. We're almost in."

With that, we grab onto the rope of soil pulling us closer to the large mound of earth ... our charms still active ... fire framing my figure and circles of light swarming around Lucy and Conrad's arms ... ready to be pulled through the earth into a silent witch's lair.

THE INTERIOR OF THE SPACE IS A SURPRISE, TO SAY THE LEAST, carpets adorning the walls and floors with a clear view of the sky on all sides. Like all magical spaces entered via Periums, the difference between the space you leave and the one you enter is striking. This space in The Royisin Heights is no different, candles on the fireplace that flicker, offering faint light.

It's as if you're standing in an open space — no sign of windows as you look out over the landscape with no sound either, meaning charms are at work to make a characterless land come to life from within. The figure who appeared in the dark outside hasn't made an appearance yet so we take the time to look around, Conrad remaining on guard whilst Lucy and I study the intricate detail of the place.

A Follygrin rests on the small table near the fire — the shelves to either side of the fireplace lined with remedies of various colours. Pink and green powder marks the floor, suggesting our absent host hasn't completely removed herself from Society business: the bottles of remedies suggesting magic is alive and well here.

Our Williynx inspect the coloured powder, maybe reminded of the role their species play in the testing of new charms, squawking if the charm is a success and passing out if it isn't. No harm done, of course.

"Who do you think she is?" Lucy asks, always keen to understand the complex family ties weaved through the S.P.M.A.

I'm less interested in *who* she is than why she's chosen to live out here. Like the Domitus in Drandok, there's a story behind each wizards and witches chosen path.

"Sit," she says, her soft voice in contrast to her general look of wildness.

She's still barefoot, dressed in a floral nightgown decorated by a silver necklace: her penchant, no doubt.

We do as she requests, taking up the three seats by the fire — as if she knew we were coming. Obviously, the fact there's three seats doesn't mean anything on its own, but then there's the silver tray on the floor near one of the chairs. Three teacups rest on the tray, each cup filled with a Society remedy: one colour for each of our penchant stones. I'd say this *isn't* a coincidence — what she says next confirming it.

"Your missing your comrade," the lady states, her long

greying hair hanging over her face as she wanders through the space, looking out at the sky.

"Noah, you mean," I reply, shrugging when Conrad gives me an impatient frown.

Conrad's much keener on *direct* action, wanting to do his duty before getting back to seeking out fun. Although this place is intriguing, *fun* doesn't describe it, meaning I've got a limited time to get information out of our host.

"Yes ... Noah, enjoying the dizzying feelings of romance in The Winter Quarter ..."

I keep my gaze on the woman, not wanting to see Lucy's reaction. To say this visit hasn't turned out the way I expected would be a mild understatement. I was expecting blistering winds and a brooding sky, trekking through The Royisin Heights and maybe bumping into a mumbling witch or wizard out on a midnight walk.

I mean, *what else* is there to do out here? Well, *plenty*, it seems, judging by the passageways, offering alternatives to a reclusive existence.

"Do you know us?" Conrad asks, tapping his feet impatiently on the concrete floor.

"Yes, Conrad; I know you. The question is, do you remember me?"

Conrad studies the face, looking for clues in the intense grey eyes. "Sorry, I don't me to be rude ... "

"Did you used to live in Society Square?" Lucy asks, a glimmer of recognition crossing her face.

The lady stops pacing, glancing towards the fire, never resting her gaze on any of us. "Yes. I lived in Society Square for many years."

"Why did you leave?"

"To unburden myself of duty."

"To the Society?"

"To my family name: a name which continued to draw unwanted attention after the last war was won."

It suddenly dawns on me who she is ... the striking grey eyes that used to be green ... the lithe figure and pretty face that Jacob was once hypnotised by. I don't know *how* I know, but I do. The mention of 'unburdening herself from family' and 'unwanted attention after the last war' makes me think of a family sharing a similar burden placed to the Renns: the Follygrin family.

The family who created the small, circular, leather-bound artefact on the table by the fire, and who also run the shop bearing their name in Founders' Quad. Francis Follygrin was the old man who provided the last piece of the puzzle: the final fragment of a lethal artefact, allowing us to rid the Society of evil intent.

It was Francis that malevs and captors sought out in the past, wondering why he'd vanished from Society life for decades, leaving people to think he was dead. It was also Francis who'd explained a life overseeing the continued imprisonment of a dark fragment in a secret cell hidden within Follygrins.

His was a life sacrificed to protect the Society, and one rejected by his granddaughter following his death. Sianna Follygrin ... changed almost beyond recognition ... the luminous eyes and voice remaining. A life forever altered by her grandfather's sacrifice.

"Sianna," I say. "Sianna Follygrin."

This gets her full attention, brushing her greying hair away from her striking face, turning her gaze onto me. "We meet in different circumstances, Guppy."

"Thanks for coming out to help us. It's pretty *wild* out here."

The first smile touches a face that was once lit with life.

"Only on the outside. You make whatever life you choose once settled here. Drink up while it's hot, then I can show you around and, perhaps, guide you on to the person you're seeking."

"So, Neve is hiding out here?" Conrad asks.

"Yes, Conrad. Neve is here but she's worked hard to create a maze around her, meaning you need to tread carefully. The one thing The Royisin Heights shares with its inhabitants is a shifting mood. Neve has no intention of being captured so, naturally, her mood will change once cornered."

"I don't suppose you've got a plan to draw her out of her?"

"Drink up," Sianna says again, the old light returning to her eyes as we do, making me hope the maze she's referring to isn't hidden in the remedy we're sipping — potentially brewed to send us off into a dreamworld where nightmares await on the other side.

23

PASSAGE TO DANGER

Thankfully, I don't wake up hours later in a dungeon with silent witches and wizards for company. The remedy tastes sweet — a blue concoction I'm not familiar with but drink anyway, confident that Sianna Follygrin remains a trusted comrade with no intention of putting us in danger.

That remains to be seen, of course, because she's suggested a path to Neve's hideout, probably accessed through one of the six passageways all leading in different directions. As the fire crackles, I glance down each passageway, seeing either darkness or glittering light, nothing else to go on so I invest in a little more patience — not my strong point — enjoying the blue remedy in my teacup until Sianna decides to tell us more.

"Have you been here long?" Lucy asks, probably trying to gain a greater understanding of our relationship with Sianna.

Lucy and Noah came into the fray after the last big battle, joining the Night Rangers when different factions formed to keep an eye on things. I rarely talk about past conflicts because you never know who's lost loved ones — each family in the S.P.M.A. having comrades and captors alike.

Take my family, for example, the Graylings. I'm a Night Ranger and Jacob's a teacher, but our mum's a Melackin now, rehabilitated after an act of betrayal. It's the same in all families: all marked in some way by shadows and sin when you take a closer look.

"Just over a year," Sianna replies, adjusting her floral dressing gown as she moves closer to us. "It feels longer but The Royisin Heights have that effect on you."

"Is that why the sky moves so quickly?" I ask, putting the teacup on the small table to my left.

"The sky is as changeable as the weather, Guppy, sometimes fast and other times completely static. Then there's the weather that can shift in minutes and form for months. I've watched blizzards morph into desert terrain in the space of a few hours."

"And you like that...? The randomness of the place, I mean?"

"That's precisely why I like it. If you remember, I lived a very *contained* life, looking after my grandfather in his secret chamber hidden within Follygrin's. It took its toll: a burden only lifted after my grandfather's death. I'm free here, unburdened by a duty that ultimately robbed my grandfather of life — a choice he made willingly, of course."

"It just seems so *remote*," Lucy adds. "*Beautiful* but silent. Does the loneliness not get to you?"

"The internal and external worlds of The Royisin Heights are vastly different, Lucy. Out there is a barren, unforgiving landscape, drawing few witches and wizards. However, inside each of these mounds of earth is a blank canvas, allowing the creation of any world imaginable: the very *freedom* I've long desired."

"And the passageways?" Conrad asks. "Are they part of your creation?"

"Of course. A blank canvas is absent of all forms, Conrad. The passageways offer me a kaleidoscope vision of my surroundings, pivoting my perspective in a multitude of ways. No two days offer the same vision — the lack of windows offering a formless connection with the outside world.

The passageway behind me leads to a stained-glass floor, looking down on the lively underground of The Royisin Heights, where those who seek comfort in company gather."

"Is that where we'll find Neve?" I ask.

"It's where she'll appear when she's unable to cope with the silence. Wherever Neve is, she's a guest in another dwelling. Of course, The Royisin Heights covers a vast distance, meaning she may appear in the underground section today, tomorrow or, perhaps, when more time has passed."

"But you think she's going to appear sooner rather than later?"

Sianna gestures to the Follygrin on the table next to my teacup — her family's invention to offer insight into a moving, mercurial world. "Her brother, Odin, is hiding between Drandok and here," she adds, "aware that Neve has sleeping soldiers on her tail."

"I thought he was using the Invisilis charm to cover his tracks?" Conrad states, moving his hands closer to the flickering fire.

"He is, but when a certain group of people change their daily rhythms, it suggests they've been called upon. Your journey here is a change in your rhythm, for example, normally gliding through the sky over The Society Sphere to more gentle realms like The Shallows. Arriving here has caused a mild commotion below."

Sianna glances at the concrete floor, signalling a moving universe beneath. I'm keen to inspect the stained-glass floor in the passageway behind her, but the offer isn't forthcoming so I rest in the leather chair, listening to the soft lilt of her voice as the sky rushes past overhead: a sky drawing our feathered friends' attention, thankful for the rest.

"Odin feels his chances are better out in the wilderness, drawing on favours or fear to find shelter. It's where the likes of Alice Aradel hide out until something draws them back to The Society Sphere — desperation or desire forcing them out of their hiding place."

"Who's offering Odin shelter?" Lucy asks, putting her teacup on the floor.

"Alice's old crew ... one of whom is Odin's cousin, Eschen Blin. The group has been wary of Odin since his training as a Domitus. I imagine he hasn't told them about his quick exit from Drandok, no longer able to ride the Silverbacks into other realms.

Odin's arrogance is his greatest weakness, meaning he will use Alice Aradel's old mob to gain access to the underground world of The Royisin Heights, where hiding in plain sight is relatively easy."

"Disfigurement charms?" I suggest, remembering Alice Aradel's deformed face when we bumped into her in Poridian Parlour. She didn't look particularly pleased to see us but, then again, neither did Joseph Flint — the eccentric wizard returning to his routine of talking to himself in The Chattering Tap.

"Indeed, Guppy. Disfigurement charms can disguise any witch or wizard. With the right contacts, you can blend in with the crowd, stretching out the days before fate closes in on you."

"But you've got the stained-glass floor," Lucy adds, glancing in the direction of the passageway, "meaning you'll know when Alice Aradel's old mob arrive — probably with someone else in tow."

"Odin," Conrad adds, standing to signal the time for action. "Can we see the stained-glass floor?"

"You can," Sianna replies, "but first you'll need to activate your Quivvens."

"Why?"

"Because, as I said, my home offers a kaleidoscope of visions, meaning there are no barriers to what lies beyond. The stained-glass floor will give you a window into underground life here; your Quivven will illuminate all other visions, formed in glass fragments buried in the walls."

Conrad's already got his Quivven out, burying the small, brass artefact into his neck. The Quivven kicks in when your penchant's powers fade — any journey beyond The Society Sphere requiring the protective and illuminate powers of a Quivven. Once buried under my heart, the artefact glows the colour of my penchant stone: a soft, topaz-blue glimmering near my heart.

Lucy places her Quivven in her forearm and we're ready to inspect the underground part of The Royisin Heights, safely cooped up in Sianna Follygrin's cosy home: a young woman who arrived here to escape a life of perpetual duty. They say once a Society soldier always a Society soldier, and I wonder if Sianna's going to find the peace she hopes for out here.

THE PASSAGEWAY WE STEP INTO REMAINS IN DARKNESS initially, our Quivvens the only thing illuminating the space. I can see the faint outline of the stained-glass floor but nothing moving beneath it. The fragments of glass buried in the walls glimmer as I turn to inspect them, understanding what Sianna meant by the need for our Quivvens.

This particular artefact has two benefits: protection and image mapping. The protection is symbolised by the glowing colours beneath our skin, the image mapping happening when we close our eyes.

I discovered the Quivven's second magical power in the throes of battle, when we entered a realm of blinding light called Varakel. The light was designed to put off visitors looking for a famous beast, blistering in its intensity to the point of critical injury if you kept your eyes open.

That's when the art of 'fighting blind' was explained to me. In times of need, your Quivven illuminates your surroundings, mapping the territory in intricate detail, meaning darkness or blistering light can be easily overcome. Standing in the dark passageway, I close my eyes and wait for my Quivven's magical powers to kick in — faint, blue light forming, stretching into fine lines.

The light settles until the fragments of glass buried into the wall become a colourful movie of a thousand parts ... each piece of glass offering a different aspect of life in The Royisin Heights. It's a unique surveillance device devised by a woman whose family created the Follygrin. Sianna is well conditioned in secrecy, understanding the link between living as a recluse and having a vantage point on the outside world.

After all, your hiding place is only as good as the security that surrounds it — Francis Follygrin knowing this better than anyone. Sianna's grandfather lived as a ghost for decades, guarding a fragment of dark sorcery in a sacrifice as great as any I know. Sianna has her own hideout now, implementing the same window onto the world that the Follygrin provides: a touch of magic offering a vision of all things magical.

I wonder if this glittering passageway looks out onto the Society as a whole, believing it probably does, allowing Sianna to stay in touch with the world she's distanced herself from. I've never understood why people don't just return to the above-ground world, having had enough of magical living. *I* couldn't but nor could I live such an isolated existence without family and friends close by.

Maybe when I'm older I'll have had enough of all things magical, although I can see myself teaching with Jacob if that happens, wanting to hold onto the coat tails of wonder. I hope that day *never* comes but you never know in life — the reason I try to squeeze every moment of joy out of each day, reminding myself that standing in a kaleidoscope passageway is *way* better than dodging curses and creatures on the battlefield.

We're only tracking down a comrade who's anger's got the better of her, meaning if she doesn't make an appearance soon we'll say our goodbyes and head back to safer realms in The Society Sphere. There's a globe-shaped building in The Winter Quarter, for instance, and a friend hoping to get his first kiss on a glittering bridge.

"Pinch your skin where the Quivven's buried," Sianna advises, "capturing the light in your hand."

I glance at Conrad and Lucy, never having heard of *this* trick before. Conrad tries it first, smiling as a tanzanite glow shimmers in his closed hand. Lucy and I do the same, copying Sianna as she kneels and places the captured colour of her Quivven onto the stained-glass floor, keeping her palm pressed down as the floor fills with light.

"Reminds me of The Floating Floor," Conrad whispers as he kneels beside me — a reference to the magical floor in The Cendryll, creating an illusion of water when you walk across it. The Floating Floor has its own secrets although my attention is firmly fixed on what's about to revealed below: the underground world of The Royisin Heights shimmering into life.

24

THE HIDDEN FEW

I study the gathering of well-dressed men and woman standing in what can only be described as a ballroom: a grand building dominated by chandeliers. A cocktail bar runs around the circumference of the underground space, drawing crowds to their preferred section. Kneeling to inspect the space more closely, I wonder what magical tonics are being mixed by the bar staff: remedies for recluses and people on the run.

Part of me wonders why the Society would allow such a place to function, blatantly offering tonics to the desperate, but that's only my perception; I imagine Sianna will tell us more in due course. There will always be places where the less savoury characters gather, either in plain sight or hide-outs such as the underground chamber of The Royisin Heights.

Society elders are not naïve enough to think peace is a permanent state of bliss; it has to be managed via monitoring and clear messaging, dealing with the wayward in a variety of ways. The glamorous space viewed through the stained-glass floor is one of these ways: a place where quiet revelry and mild mischief are managed until judgement arrives in the form of Night Rangers or sleeping soldiers.

Judgement is closing in on Neve and Odin so there's no need to rush into an unfamiliar place, so I decide to sit cross-legged on the floor, studying every figure who enters and leaves, wondering what disguise Neve is using to hide her movements. There's also Alice Aradel's old mob to look out for: Eschen Blin, Roland Gupp, Morval Crake and Golen Rais.

Eschen is the most likely to make an appearance — the cousin of Odin and Neve who, according to Sianna, has provided Odin with shelter with the aim to conceal him in the shifting world of figures visible through a stained-glass floor. They obviously can't see us looking down at them because no-one looks up. I also wonder if they can hear us due to Sianna explaining how each cocktail of remedies disfigures in different ways: temporarily, of course.

You could say this secret hideout is the perfect place for the creative witch or wizard, able to use their imagination and wit to evade those tracking them down. Unfortunately for Odin and Neve, we've bumped into an old comrade on our arrival in The Royisin Heights — Sianna Follygrin — as skilled as anyone in the art of covert movements.

If Sianna has created a way to observe her surroundings, I'm confident she also knows the best way into the underground ballroom, hosting a crowd of well-groomed witches and wizards.

"How do you find who you're looking for?" Lucy asks, sitting alongside me on the stained-glass floor.

"You study the extent of the disguise and ease of movement," Sianna replies, pointing to an example of this theory. "The lady who has just arrived to our right. Her make-up is lightly applied but the hair isn't her own ... her pale, freckled complexion suggesting a redhead hiding within a mass of black hair. Secondly, she heads straight to the cocktail bar nearest to her — the rash remedies section — giving you the desired disfigurement in one gulp."

"So, what does that tell us?" Conrad asks, tapping his feet as he considers Sianna's method of identifying Society targets.

"That she's arrived here in a hurry, maybe unsuccessful in securing shelter along the way. Remember, most inhabitants of The Royisin Heights seek peace and sanctuary, having no interest in engaging with others. The people you see below aren't part of this group who live in the mounds of earth decorating the landscape. They are the moving feast ... entering and exiting through the four doorways to seek transformation and configuration."

"Configuration?" I query, managing to suppress a sneeze.

"Adapting their plans to lengthen their time here," Sianna replies, "normally meaning entering into deals with those offering shelter and passage to wilder realms."

"Who are the people who offer the deals?"

"The Domitus until recently ... Odin and Neve arriving on their tamed Silverbacks to intimidate and negotiate ... transporting the desperate to remote realms for a price."

"Like Alice Aradel," Lucy adds.

"Yes, Lucy," Sianna replies as she clicks her fingers, causing the stained-glass floor to fade away. "Alice arrived here some time ago, realising her time was up in Society Square. Luckily, she hadn't carried out any serious crime— the rumour of her planned kidnapping of your young wizarding crew being hard to prove.

There's no way back to the heart of the S.P.M.A. for Alice, however, meaning an increased reliance on groups like The Domitus to keep her hidden: a plan that only ever had a certain amount of life."

With the stained-glass floor disappearing from view, Sianna gestures for us to follow her along the passageway, the shards of glass illuminated by the Quivvens glowing underneath our skin. We reach a wider space soon afterwards, opening out into an extension of the decorative feature of the passageway: shards of glass glimmering around us ... each one offering insight into the different shades of The Royisin Heights.

All we have to do now is close our eyes and allow our Quivvens to go to work, mapping the territory hidden within the shards of glass, seeking out a Domitus on the run, hiding in plain sight: a cocktail of remedies transforming her features in the hope that freedom will last a little longer.

With my eyes closed, the surrounding space glitters into life ... the glass shards spinning in the walls until one fragment catches my attention ... a group moving on foot in the darkness ... Drandok in the distance.

"Alice Aradel's old mob," I say, pointing to the fragment in question.

Conrad and Lucy huddle closer, turning their attention to the spinning glass shard illuminated by our Quivvens. Lucy isn't familiar with Alice Aradel but Conrad is, pointing out Eschen Blin who leads the group. Eschen guides a figure who walks with his coat pulled over his head, protecting himself from the swirling wind. It's his first mistake, the conditions not severe enough to require a cover for his face: Odin Blin.

Odin's relying on his cousin, Eschen, to get him to the underground sanctuary of The Royisin Heights, assuming it to be a place where he can hide for a while — just as Alice

Aradel had done quite successfully for some time. The Society wasn't actively looking for Aradel, though, judging her crimes insignificant in contrast to those who had killed and maimed in war.

Odin and Neve's crimes aren't at that level, either, but Society rules are clear: any attack on another comrade has consequences, and the two Domitus who started this dance in Poridian Parlour are in for some bad news — about to discover their hideout can be viewed through a certain looking glass, courtesy of a witch with a gift for ghosting. The witch in question disappears moments after we've tracked down Odin.

"Where's she gone?" Lucy asks, turning her attention away from the spinning glass shards.

I look down the passageway, seeing nothing but the blue light of my Quivven, realising that Sianna has done her duty, guiding us to the location of the two people we seek. We're in danger of outstaying our welcome so we decide to move on.

We whistle for our Williynx, watching as they glide through the passageway, settling by our feet, about to take us back into the air on the track of a desperate Domitus. The only thing left to do is work out the best way of exiting Sianna's home. A Cympgus is the obvious option, providing a portable Perium of light for us to step through, but it's always fun to work out the unique transportation methods of new places.

"It's probably an incantation only known to Sianna," Conrad suggests, kneeling to stroke Erivan's turquoise feathers.

"Sianna wouldn't have left us if we needed that," Lucy counters, rubbing her hands on her jeans. "It'll be something straightforward."

"Such as?"

"Tapping the shard of glass that showed us Odin's position," I reply, keeping my eyes closed as the Quivven floods the space with bright light.

"Well, let's try it," Conrad states, leading the three of us to step closer to the spinning fragment.

We reach out to tap the shard of glass, watching as it separates itself from the wall, floating above us.

"What if it tries to stab us?" Lucy asks, putting a hand over her face just in case.

I smile at the thought of this. "A killer glass shard; it would be a funny way to die."

"You've got a morbid mind, Guppy."

"And you need to lighten up."

"Well, if it *does* attack us I'll look out for your laughter."

"*Okay, ladies*," Conrad interrupts, itching to get back into the air, "let's get on with it. We've got a Domitus to catch."

I leave the little spat with Lucy, conscious she's got Noah's date on her mind. "I say we catch the glass fragment, like we caught our Quivven's light. It fits to the method Sianna used to illuminate the stained-glass floor."

"I'm in," Conrad said, a look of urgency on his face.

"Let's go," Lucy adds, and we reach up together, slowly placing our hands around the spinning glass shard.

I feel the glass graze my palm until a blanket of light falls over us, covering our bodies at the same time our Williynx rise up towards the source of light, shape shifting into larger forms as they do.

"Grab on," Conrad urges, reaching for Erivan as his feathered companion glides towards the high ceiling, squawking to signal our impending exit.

I jump onto Laieya, checking to make sure Lucy is

behind me — the three of us exiting Sianna's secret chamber, ready to blast into action once more.

We appear in the sky above The Royisin Heights, using the Verum Veras charm to hide our movements. Odin and his crew will be looking out for danger, probably firing desperate charms into the air if they spot us, so caution is necessary. There's no plan for another fire fight but this could be unavoidable, depending on Odin's reaction. One thing is certain: he isn't going to make it to The Royisin Heights.

Conrad hands me a vial of white liquid called Semphul: a remedy for hunger on busy evenings of Night Ranging. Gulping it down in one go, I keep my eyes on the terrain below, waiting for Odin to appear. There's nothing to say he isn't using an invisibility charm as well now, possibly catching a glimpse of us appearing in the air before I suggested stealth was necessary.

It's possible although we're still some distance from his location, according to Sianna's unique surveillance device buried in her walls. It's more likely he's using the darkness to stay out of sight or, less promising, has found another way to accelerate his journey. The Disira charm is always an option, allowing you to vanish to your chosen location, but it would be dangerous under the circumstances.

Odin knows he's being tracked and is skilled enough in battle strategy to know the flaws of the Disira charm. It's a quick means of escape but you don't know who you're going to bump into on the other side, so he's stuck with natural travel for now, and I wonder if he's regretting his visit to Poridian Parlour a few nights ago, calling out a young crew of wizards who don't back down from a challenge.

~

WE FINALLY CATCH SIGHT OF ODIN LESS THAN A MILE FROM The Royisin Heights, walking with Alice Aradel's old mob who do their best to provide cover. Odin walks in the middle of the group, his coat no longer lifted over his head. Instead, he's used a disfigurement charm to mark the left side of his face — nothing extreme but enough to pass without being spotted, particularly to recluses largely uninterested in the movements of Society members.

We've got a vested interest, of course, so formulate the plan of attack, agreeing on the element of surprise. We're still hidden behind the Verum Veras charm, the glittering interior curtain of light hiding us from view until we decide to reacquaint ourselves with Odin.

I doubt he's going to react well so I whisper to Laieya, her powder-blue feathers lifting in recognition of my plan. I've got fire and Laieya's got ice, meaning Odin doesn't stand a chance. That's what you get when you mess with The Fire Witch.

Conrad signals for us to go lower, descending slowly on our target while we ready our surprise. Flight is Conrad's trusted mode of engagement, rarely activating defensive charms unless the situation becomes critical. He's an elusive target in the air, having a particular affinity with Erivan — his turquoise Williynx who darts in and out of the rhythms he orchestrates.

Lucy combines charms at speed, usually relying on the Promesiun charm before adding water or fire to her blasts of light and energy. Together, we're a pretty formidable force, surrounding the target on all sides until they submit or fire back, which is when things get interesting.

We'll soon find out how desperate Odin is, aware the Domitus are proud soldiers. Damaged, yes, but proud, so it's unlikely Odin's going to submit without a fight.

"I'll take care of Aradel's mob," Conrad says as we descend lower, "You and Lucy make sure Odin doesn't get away."

I nod as the wind lifts suddenly, whipping my hair back. Lucy's cropped black hair gives her fewer problems, yellow ribbons of light spinning around her arms in preparation for contact with the target.

"And if they fire back?" Lucy asks, her hands placed around her Williynx's neck.

"A prison of ice bullets," I reply, already envisioning the cage to trap Odin and his crew in. Ice makes the enemy scatter, but *ice bullets* are something else altogether. It's the weapon to end all arguments although serious injury hasn't been authorised, meaning Odin's about to step into a taming range of a different kind.

"Take out one of Aradel's mob first," Conrad adds, a natural leader in the sky, "Send them running for cover, creating the panic we need. The rest will be easy. Let's go."

With that, we tap our ankles against our Williynx and accelerate towards the small crew of malevs, their hopes increasing as they close in on The Royisin Heights. That's until they see a blast of colour in the sky above them ... too shocked to react quickly enough, scrambling to fire a volley of charms to distract us from our mission.

Lucy and I veer off in opposite directions, drawing the attention of Odin's crew who scatter as streaks of light explode into the soil around their feet. An avalanche of water follows, sending the hapless crew careering along on a water slide that threatens to submerge them.

With Odin's mob taken care of, Conrad adds the finishing touches to our evening, whispering for Erivan to expand into a colossal form, the turquoise creature spreading its wings to signal the fury it's about to unleash.

Erivan's roar is enough to snap Odin into action, the frightened look on his face turning to surprise as Conrad falls from his Williynx, spinning towards the stranded Domitus with no protective curtain or active charm: a blatant statement of superiority designed to test the level of venom buried in Odin.

Domitus are soldiers haunted by war, after all, recuperating in Drandok until they recover or falter, Odin's raised arm putting him in the latter category. He's fallen into Conrad's trap, yelling in fury as he shouts 'SALIX': the first and last time he'll use an unauthorised curse on active duty.

As the energy changes around us, I whip the Levenan charm into a more furious rhythm, ensuring the two malevs in my grasp get the most out of the unforgiving waterfall they're trapped in. They'll live to tell the tale in The Velynx.

With Lucy doing the same, I glance back to see Conrad vanishing in the air ... a step ahead of Odin who tries to catch his disappearing figure, but he's trapped in ways he doesn't understand yet, too consumed by his anger to notice Erivan shape-shifting above him ... the turquoise Williynx breathing flumes of white mist that signal the conclusion to this dance.

As Odin spins around, shouting for Conrad to show himself, Erivan flutters into a tiny form, releasing a flurry of feathers near the Domitus's feet ... feathers that turn into spirals of light, wrapping around Odin's body. He tries to whip out the curse again, realising he's instigated his own demise seconds later ... the Salix curse rebounding and ripping through his body, sending him collapsing to the earth.

Erivan releases a second flurry of feathers, guiding them over the gaping wound almost detaching Odin's right shoulder from his body. With his crew floating unconscious in the surge of water, I watch as Odin's wound heals: another touch of magic from our feathered friends.

As Odin grunts in pain, I fire a Promesiun charm into the air, twisting my wrist as it rises to ensure the blue light washes the sky: a call to the sleeping soldiers tasked with transporting targets to The Velynx.

Thankfully, crossing Quibbs Causeway isn't part of our remit, meaning we can leave a party with the Mantzils to our comrades — comrades conditioned to cope with the mind-piercing screech of the Mantzils: one Society creature I *don't* miss.

25

HEALING VISITS

We return to The Society Sphere after a group of sleeping soldiers arrive to take care of Odin and his crew. Our duty as Night Rangers is done so it's time to squeeze the final bit of life out of the evening, my thoughts returning to Noah's date with Zoe. Part of me hopes it's gone well with the other part still uncertain of Zoe's motives.

From never giving Noah any signs of interest to suddenly agreeing to go on a date still seems a bit odd, but people *can* be odd, including me. I also need to remember that it took me a while to recognise my bond with Conrad was more than friendship, so this could be what's playing out between Noah and Zoe.

If we fly past The Winter Quarter, we'll know how the date's gone, but I don't want to bring this up. I've grown out of my impulsive phase, realising where it can lead, which doesn't mean I don't struggle with a desire to jump into things without thinking them through.

Surprisingly, it's Lucy who brings up the idea of flying over The Winter Quarter, suggesting we should check on

Noah. We all know what 'checking on Noah' means but I see it as a good sign: at least she's not out for Zoe's blood.

"If Noah's had any luck, they should be on The Sinking Bridge by now," Conrad says, moving his attention from Lucy's needs to Noah's.

Noah's one of Conrad's closest friends so it's natural for him to hope for the best, choosing his words carefully to avoid upsetting Lucy.

"Or they could still be in Velerin's," I add, patting Laieya in recognition of her tiredness.

"I've never seen Zoe out after midnight," Lucy comments, "so they'll be on The Sinking Bridge or heading back to The Singing Quarter."

"Well, let's go and find out," I add, tapping my ankles to signal a need for speed.

I'm keen to end the night with a bit of fun, wishing Sianna Follygrin well in her hideaway in The Royisin Heights. Maybe that will be me one day, checking out quieter realms, but there's *way* too much fun to still be had, starting with the lowdown on Noah's date and whether he's managed to sneak in the long-hoped for kiss.

~

We find Noah on The Sinking Bridge but not in the company of Zoe who, he says, had to leave early.

"What do you mean *early*?" Conrad asks, checking on his friend as Lucy and I give them some space.

"Straight after the meal," Noah replies, looking handsome in his purple suit, the gold pocket watch open in his hand.

He's using the watch to avoid eye contact with us — a sign he's struggling with his emotions. Noah's not much of a crier but goes silent when he's upset, meaning we need to tread carefully.

"Did it go well?" I ask, sensing the answer.

"It went fine," Noah replies, but his tone suggests it didn't. "We mainly talked about night ranging. You know, what we get up to."

"Did you talk about *you*?" Lucy asks. "I mean, the two of you."

Noah shakes his head, rubbing the edges of the gold pocket watch. "I've been an idiot."

"Easy, Noah," Conrad offers, placing an arm around his friend's shoulder. "You still got your date."

"Yeah, the only one I'm going to get."

"Did Zoe say that?"

"She didn't have to ..."

Conrad looks over to us, gesturing for help which I leave to Lucy, sensing she needs some alone time with Noah now.

"He looks a bit a crushed," I say as Conrad reaches me.

"He is. He really likes her."

"I know."

"Making it harder for Lucy who *really likes him*."

"If only he could see that."

"He's sort of lost in the *idea* of Zoe, I think," Conrad adds, keeping a watchful eye over Noah who offers a sad smile as Lucy perches alongside him. "He'll need time to realise that the idea and the reality don't match. Zoe's *cold* ... not cruel but *removed* ... *definitely not* what Noah needs."

It's rare for Conrad to comment negatively on others. Having lost both parents, he always looks for the positive in relationships, acutely aware of how quickly they can expire. He's right, though, Zoe has a detached quality, making her a perfect barmaid but not girlfriend material — at least not for Noah who needs to feel wanted.

Like my brother Jacob, Noah didn't have the best start in the S.P.M.A. and has had to work to prove himself, most importantly to his dad who's got his own superiority complex. It's possible Zoe reminds Noah of his dad, subconsciously at least, which is something he'll hopefully work through in time.

The glimmer of light is the first sign of a closer bond between Lucy and Noah ... each of them placing their penchants on the bridge, decorating it in their combined colours. I watch as a vision of yellow and green illuminate the bridge, lighting up the quiet streets of The Winter Quarter.

The bridge shimmers in the way Noah hoped it would with Zoe, but instead he's got the love of the friend to complete his date: a friend who suggests stronger feelings through gestures rather than words. There's no doubt letting your guard down is *scary* — I'll be the first to admit that — so I stand with Conrad, smiling as Lucy finally gets a laugh out of Noah, hoping they'll give each other a chance of love one day.

The glittering colour decorating the bridge doesn't extend to the water: a sign they'll only ever be friends or that Noah's love for Lucy hasn't yet ignited. Time will tell, either way. The final touch of colour appears in the sky: a vision of red arriving with healing powers only a Williynx can offer. Noah looks up in surprise at the sight of his fire-red companion descending from the night sky, arriving to offer reassurance and comfort.

"We're lucky," I say, leaning into Conrad for a hug. "Lucky to have all this."

"*Amazingly* lucky," Conrad adds, "and I'm lucky to have you."

"I know," I reply with a flirtatious smile, getting the

expected laugh from Conrad. "Let's end the night with a race — get Noah's blood boiling in a different way."

Conrad laughs again, placing an arm around my waist as he calls over to Noah and Lucy. "Last one back to Founders' Quad has to check on Odin in The Velynx."

That gets everyone moving — The Velynx located at the end of Quibbs Causeway where the Mantzils live: a place we can all navigate but never choose to. I mean, who wants a splitting headache for a week?

Conrad's already in the air, dipping down to glide over the water, the claws of his Williynx touching the water. "Come on lover boy!" Conrad calls out to Noah, pleased his friend has snapped out of his moment of self-pity. "Night Rangers don't rest! Unless you've missed the Mantzils, that is."

That's enough to kick Noah into action, following close behind Lucy as the four us form a line, gliding across the water running under The Sinking Bridge that glimmers in the evening light. I let out a yelp of laughter as Laieya joins in the fun, spinning me three times as she rises higher, trying to get ahead of Conrad who responds by going *under water* on Erivan, reappearing *way ahead of us.*

"*Cheating!*" Noah calls out, his purple suit jacket whipping in the wind, soft flakes of snow falling over his hair and clothes.

The old Noah's back now, singing whilst patting his fire-red companion into furious flight: a friend appreciating another form of love.

~

A FEW WEEKS PASS UNTIL WE REACH THE DAY MUM MENTIONED on my last visit: Jacob's birthday. I promised I'd be there and

Jacob's reminded me of it loads of times. My brother's been there more for me more than anyone else in my life, so I'm not going to miss his birthday although how it's going to play out at mum's is another question.

It's Jacob's idea to have his birthday party at mum's — a chance to rebuild a bond that I still think is permanently broken. I'm less forgiving than my brother, believing some sins are unforgivable. Either way, today's not about me so I collect the present and card from my bed, preparing to meet Conrad on the ground floor of The Cendryll.

Thoughts on family always send me into a bit of a spin, so I've spent the morning on the fourth floor, preparing myself for a return to the twisted building on the margins of Society Square. Returning there always makes me think of Isiah Renn and the sacrifices he made for the Society, including leaving his house to mum — not something she necessarily deserves.

The expected sound comes from my bedside table, my Scribberal signalling new communication. A Scribberal is the main communication device in the Society: a silver container you receive notes and letters in. It's a secure way of keeping things *in house*, meaning no above-ground trickery can access any communication travelling within our secret world.

I lift the lid of the Scribberal to see the note from Jacob. *We're waiting by The Seating Station* the note reads. It's Jacob's way of saying 'hurry up' so I check my hair in the mirror and leave the bedroom, heading for the ground floor.

~

"READY?" JACOB ASKS, MEETING ME BY THE LIFT WITH Conrad.

I decided taking the spiral staircase would probably lead to a lot of polite hellos, making me even later — not the best start to your brother's birthday.

"Yep."

"What's the present?" Jacob asks with a smile, no longer wearing the tie required for teaching duties.

He's asked Farraday to look after his class: a scarred Society legend with more magic in his little finger than most have in their entire repertoire. I've got a soft spot for Farraday: the man who trained me and saved my life on more than one occasion.

"Are we staying long?" I ask.

"*Guppy*," comes Conrad's reply.

"Let's just enjoy the day, okay?" Jacob adds, his tired expression suggesting the challenges his class is posing.

He needs my support so I park my self-centred concerns, linking arms with my brother. I offer him a smile as the three of us head towards the closest Perium, situated behind The Seating Station. We'll be at mum's in less than five minutes.

~

MY MUM IS MORE ENGAGING ON THIS VISIT, CLEARLY GOING TO a lot of effort to make Jacob feel special. She's made a lot of mistakes but I know I need to get over this, learning that judging every mistake people make forces you to look at your own flaws, and I've got plenty.

The presents remain on the kitchen table, bringing a smile to my face every time Jacob glances at them. His attention is always on the needs of others, even on his birthday. He checks in on Conrad, offering him more cake and Jysyn Juice, only stopping when I give him a look.

He's the kindest person I know, finally the focus of a birthday party without tension or resentment: a unique experience in the Grayling household.

"Are you going to open your presents?" mum asks as she cuts more cake — a vision of maternal attentiveness that gives me hope for the future.

"When I get home," Jacob replies, referring to his fifth-floor quarters in The Cendryll.

"You can't open them when you get home," I challenge. "We need to watch; it's part of the fun."

"Just in case you don't like mine, Guppy chose it," Conrad adds with a mischievous look in my direction.

"I'm sure I'll love them all," Jacob replies, finally relenting and reaching for the presents.

The rule on presents is no magic: one of the few situations where the above-ground world triumphs. It's not much fun getting an artefact or a book on charms: things we see every day. Presents are meant to be *novel* — unique and unexpected — so the most boring, ordinary presents are the best ones.

Jacob opens my present first, building up the tension as he unwraps the box in slow motion. "I bet it's a watch," he says, smiling in anticipation. "A bracelet ..."

He inspects the bracelet, making sure I haven't broken the no-magic rule, which I haven't. It's an ordinary silver bracelet except for one thing: the photograph hidden in the small compartment you click open. Jacob works this out after a few seconds, taking care to work the compartment open — his expression softening at the sight of the photograph inside. "It's perfect," he says, staring at the photo until mum asks to have a look at the bracelet.

The tiny photograph is of the three of us — Jacob, mum and me — sitting in the above-ground house we lived in until I was thirteen. It's a picture I've kept all these years, keeping it hidden away in various drawers. I thought Jacob's birthday was a perfect time to get it back out, fixing it in a place where it would always be visited.

Mum studies the photo in silence, running a finger over it as if she's struggling to recognise herself. It's where we once were and are struggling to return to, but if Jacob's willing to try so should I.

Conrad watches the intimate moment, probably thinking of a family he no longer has: a constant reminder to be thankful for what I've got. As I help Jacob to put the bracelet on, mum goes into the kitchen to make more tea, thanking us for coming as she does: a step in the right direction.

~

WITH PRESENTS OPENED AND THE KITCHEN TABLE CLEARED, A few games are played until mum and Jacob start to fade, leading us to say our goodbyes as the afternoon sun rests on the horizon. Cympgus' will transport us back to The Cendryll, although Conrad seems set on a different idea.

"I'll leave you here," Jacob says, offering hugs as he utters 'Whereabouts' to generate a portal Perium. "Thanks for the presents and drop by more often: the students love seeing you."

"What about tomorrow?" Conrad offers. "Round Two of Rucklz."

"You're on," Jacob replies as he walks up the glowing steps, vanishing into thin air.

With Jacob on the way back to The Cendryll, Conrad turns to me with a familiar look of mischief in his eyes.

"I know that look," I say, sensing his plan.

"What look?" he replies as he generates his own Cympgus: a glittering bridge stretching ahead of us. "I say we see where the bridge leads, and leave Noah and Lucy to the night ranging later. You never know, it might help Lucy to express her feelings for Noah."

I smile at the idea of another day of discovery with Conrad, hoping our friends find something more than shifty witches and wizards on their evening travels. You can't force love but there's nothing wrong with giving it a helping hand, and I think Lucy will appreciate the alone time with Noah.

We'll also need to track down Neve Blin soon but that can wait for another day, so I park thoughts of dangerous Domitus and take Conrad's hand, stepping onto the shimmering bridge, stretching as far as the eye can see — ready to transport us to wherever our hearts desire.

TEASER CHAPTER BOOK 2

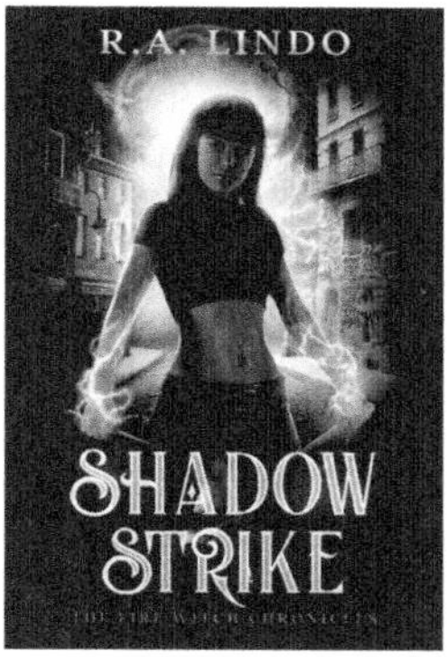

Merrymopes milkshake and ice cream parlour rests quietly in the evening light. We're preparing to start night duties on the trail of Neve Blin, the reason we're here instead of Pat's Caff — the usual meeting point for Night Rangers. Noah's got himself embroiled in another bet, throwing more Kyals at the likely hiding place of Neve Blin.

Rumour has it the ex Domitus is holed up in The Royisin Heights, blending into the underground world there with the help of a disfigurement charm. Conrad isn't arguing that Neve *isn't* there; his bet is that she won't be when we finally catch up with her.

I don't care either way and, thankfully, neither does Lucy, rolling her eyes at me as Noah and Conrad argue on the stake they're willing to bet, deciding on an arm wrestling contest to decide things. It looks like we're in for a long night.

The Merrymope twins who run the place are parked away on the upper floors of a building as colourful as its owners — red and white running along the walls and furniture. Like Pat's Caff, Merrymopes has normal hours and Night Ranger hours: a welcome dose of tranquillity for the exhausted society soldier.

The four of us sit in the private booth sectioned off from the main customer area, out of sight of prying eyes. Now, it's just a case of passing the time before duty calls, taking us to The Royisin Heights. With the arm wrestling in full swing, I study my Follygrin, hoping to catch sight of Neve Blin, but she's mastered whatever disguise she's using.

With no sign of the Domitus in hiding, I turn my attention to Lucy. She's been unusually quiet recently, probably due to her hidden feelings for Noah. Not as hidden as they once were after Zoe Tallis brought the first tinges of jealously to the fore. Lucy's pretty and funny but a bit of a mystery in the romantic realm of things.

I wasn't sure she even liked boys until Noah finally got a date with Zoe Tallis. We don't talk about 'the date' although that hasn't stopped us hanging out in Rebel's Rest which opens until the early hours. Noah does his best to ignore Zoe when we're there now, and the four of us avoid the topic altogether.

There's always something going on to keep us occupied,

the current whereabouts of Neve Blin to current dilemma we're facing.

"You'll be out of Kyals soon, the way you're going on," Conrad comments, finally winning the arm wrestle.

"Getting cold feet?" Noah prompts, spinning his Vaspyl in his hand.

The Vaspyl transforms from a small, silver horse to a candle for our table: a nice touch improved by Lucy's utterance of 'Flori', adding flowers to the table.

"A romantic dinner for four," Noah jokes, drawing laughter from us all.

Conrad sits alongside me in the leather booth. I'm in my Night Ranger uniform of black leather trousers and top of the same colour. It's the look I adopted when people started calling me The Fire Witch. I like the name so stick to my all-black attire, adding a bit of style to our evening travels.

"So, you definitely want to bet we find Neve in The Royisin Heights?" Conrad asks again, concerned Noah's getting hooked on betting at every opportunity.

"Yep. Where else is she going to go?"

"Anywhere she can hide," Lucy counters, tapping her feet on the red-and-white striped floor.

"Then place your bets," Noah encourages, brushing his floppy fringe away from his eyes.

"I can't take any more money off you; it's embarrassing," Lucy teases.

"I'll take the bet," Conrad agrees, "but only if you don't sulk when I win."

"*Deal*," Noah says with a smile, offering a handshake before he locks Conrad in another arm wrestle, the friends adding a touch of magic with the flight charm — flowers wrapping around their hands that lift them off their feet.

Lucy rolls her eyes, trying to hide the fact her attention's on Noah. He's clearly the boy she wants and with Zoe Tallis out of picture, she might just get her chance. She laughs at the sight of Conrad and Noah spinning in mid-air together, holding hands as if they're perfecting a dance: an arm wrestle turning into a comedy act. Neve Blin returns to my thoughts as the morning light falls over Society Square.

My money's on her staying put in The Royisin Heights, probably regretting her choice of tempting us into a duel. Friendly duels are okay but our little fire fight in Drandok wasn't of the friendly kind. No doubt, Neve will have another surprise in store when we finally track her down.

With Conrad and Noah over their mid-air wrestling match, we prepare to leave Merrymopes for The Royisin Heights. No door is needed to make this journey this morning, Merrymopes offering its own unique Perium to all Society realms. I place my penchant bracelet on the brass edge of the booth we're sitting in, listening to the bell ringing on the counter.

It rings of its own accord again, causing the entire room to shudder as the red-and-white leather booth descends through the gap beneath our feet. Once we get lower, we see the familiar sight of a large, circular room revolving at speed.

The only other thing in the room is the brass barrier framing it, stopping people from getting injured when they mistime their jump. The Revolving Room is another wonder of the S.P.M.A., a unique Perium accessible to the chosen few.

I used it a lot in my early days when being an underage witch was more of a problem. Then, it was advisable to travel unseen, particularly if I wasn't in the company of adults which was always the aim. Secret travel isn't required now but I still like the thrill of certain Periums: The Revolving Room being one them.

The fun is in jumping on and staying on, the room spinning so quickly it's easy to mistime your jump and be sent flying. There's a way of slowing the room down, though, which is what Conrad does now by placing his penchant ring on the iron dock we're standing on.

We time our jump as the spinning structure gathers speed, making our way to the middle where a brass dial waits to transport us to our destination. Instead of doing this, we stay on longer than needed, laughing as the room tilts and throws us off balance. The Fixilia charm takes care of this, freezing us to the spot.

"The first person to move buys the Jysyn Juice tonight," Conrad prompts, causing us to lock into Night Ranger mode: intense and still as The Revolving Room clatters in the surrounding space. We all remain perfectly still until The Revolving Room jolts suddenly, throwing Noah forwards with a yell of frustration.

"*Every time*!" he shouts, referring to his streak of bad luck on recent bets.

He can drown his sorrows with Jysyn Juice later. We've got an ex Domitus in hiding to track down.

"Let's go," I say, as we deactivate our Fixilia charms.

I reach for the brass dial in the centre of the spinning structure, dialling the required letters. Seconds later, the expected image forms in one of the doorways — the signal to move towards it and jump through: Night Rangers on a mission to tie up loose ends.

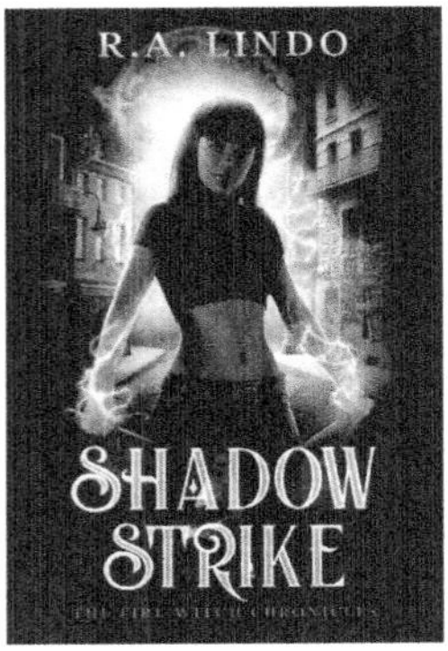

Buy Book 2

ABOUT THE AUTHOR

I'm the author of the **Kaira Renn** series, **The Fire Witch Chronicles** and **Magic & Misdemeanours**, all set in The Society for the Preservation of Magical Artefacts. (S.P.M.A.)

If you enjoyed the book, please consider **leaving a review on Amazon.**

To receive updates and a chance to win free copies of future titles, sign up to my newsletter **here**.

You can also join my **Facebook group** dedicated the S.P.M.A. universe.

ALSO BY R.A. LINDO

THE S.P.M.A. UNIVERSE

5 books per series

Kaira Renn Series: origin series

The Fire Witch Chronicles: spin-off series one

Magic & Misdemeanours: spin-off series two

Printed in Great Britain
by Amazon

21007379R00139